NEW MEXICO

A Novel of the Old West

by

Bert Entwistle

Published and printed in the United States of America, Colorado Springs, Colorado, 80918
All books available at amazon.com, bookstores the publisher:

Black Mule Press:
westernimages@msn.com
(719) 287-8063

Copyright © 2016 Bert Entwistle
First edition, November 2016, revisions 2022

ISBN 978-0-9896761-5-1
Library of Congress Control Number: 2016919373

Cover photo: working cowboy Jerry King,
Photographed on Grand Mesa Colorado
by Bert Entwistle

Cover design by Donald R. Kallaus

This book is for all my grandkids

and great grandkids. . .

You can read it on one of your e-devices.

Books by Bert Entwistle

The Drift
Jack Bannister mystery #1

Uranium Drive-In
Jack Bannister mystery #2

The Taylor Legacy,
An American Family Saga

The Black Rose Banker

Murder in the Dell

New Mexico,
A Novel of the Old West

Leftover Soldiers,
Book 1, Life on the Western Frontier

Leftover Soldiers,
Book 2, Aftermath & Opportunity

Looking Back,
Stories of Real American Pioneers

Author's Note

The main character of the lawman, José Taylor, comes from my books; Uranium Drive-In and The Taylor Legacy, both about New Mexico and Colorado. This is my first traditional western novel like those I'd been reading about and watching on the screen since I was a little kid. I tried to tell a story that was similar to writers like Louie Lamour and Zane Grey but slightly updated in style.

In 1966, as a newly minted 18 year-old high school graduate, two of my high school buddies and I piled into an old Chevy and headed to the land of the Wild West of my youth, and I was hooked for life. When we hit the Rocky Mountains I knew I would end up somewhere in this part of the world. We came back through New Mexico and it cemented my future plans permanently. All I could think about was when will I get back. Before long, another of my old friends mentioned he wanted to see Yellowstone and we were planning the next trip. By the time we got back home from that trip, the bug to move to the West was chewing on me pretty bad.

I grew up in the small town of Rochelle Illinois, in the middle of the corn belt, and I was not a corn farmer. Many of my friends were involved in farming and have enjoyed a good life because of it. But for me, I felt that if I stayed I would always miss out on the western life I dreamed of. It took until 1974, with my beautiful (and understanding) wife Nancy, and two small sons, but I finally was able to move from Illinois to Colorado. For me, it was the right thing to do. After all these years I am still carrying on a love affair with the American West. I live in Colorado, but New Mexico is never far from my mind and that's why I love to write about it. Even today a trip through New Mexico has a sense of history and adventure about it that is special. Driving through the state you can feel the history of volcanoes, Indians, pioneers, cattle drives, outlaws and shootouts like nowhere else I've ever been. I try and capture the real feeling of this special place; I hope you like the story.

Bert Entwistle
Colorado Springs, Colorado, October, 2016

Chapter 1

Tying his horse in the cedars, José took off his spurs, hat and gun belt and hung them on the saddle horn. Dropping down on his hands and knees, he crawled the hundred yards to the edge of the broken rimrock with his rifle across his arms. Belly-crawling the last few feet through the dirt, he ignored the prickly pear cactus and sharp rocks tearing at him.

Peering through an opening in the sage, he saw two men sitting in the bottom of the narrow canyon. Their horses were picketed on a long rope and their saddles lay on opposite sides of a small fire. He carried warrants for both of them. One was wanted for the murder of a Chinese farmer. The other was wanted for stealing a pair of Hereford bulls from a rancher south of Magdalena.

He'd been on the killer's trail for three days, to find the other man with him was a lucky coincidence. Checking the warrant one more time, it said the murderer was left-handed. The biggest man looked like the picture on the poster, tall and heavyset, he carried a revolver tucked into the right side of his waistband, an easy reach for a lefthander. A rifle lay on the ground next to him and a shotgun lay next to the bull thief, an older Mexican man, thick in the middle with graying hair.

1

Picking his way through the loose rocks and patches of mesquite bush and down a narrow side canyon, he followed it into the main one just below the men. When he got to where he could see them, he picked up a rock, and gave it a hard throw toward the horses. Hitting the front one on the neck caused it to rear back and spook the other one. Thrashing and kicking, they jerked the picket rope free and bolted down the canyon in a ball of dust past the outlaws.

Both men leaped up, cursed the horses and took up the chase, leaving their long guns behind. As they reached Taylor, he stepped out and pointed his Winchester at them. Stop right there and raise your hands. I am Deputy Sheriff José Taylor; you are both under arrest."

The Mexican man had his hands as high as he could get them, palms forward and fingers spread wide. "Please do not shoot, señor, I have no weapon, only the one shotgun and it is back by the fire."

"Stay just like that. Move one inch and I will kill you."

"Sí, sí, no problema, I am going nowhere."

While Taylor spoke to the thief, he had the Winchester leveled at the big man, staring straight into his eyes. "I said put your hands up high — I will not say it again."

"Ain't no way you'd shoot me just standin' here like this." Looking into Taylor's unblinking eyes with the muzzle of his Winchester so close, convinced him to raise his hands.

"With your right hand, remove the pistol and toss it behind you." Only ten feet from the man, the rifle sight never left his chest as the gun landed in the dirt. "Now, both hands behind your back and turn around slow," said Taylor, tossing his shackles to the Mexican. "Bull thief, take these and hook him up behind his back, tight. Then go and find the horses. You try to run; I will kill you."

"Sí, I will do, Señor." After gathering up the horses, he saddled them and helped Taylor get the big man on the horse. Then he mounted his own.

"Bull thief, here is what you will do. You go first and keep the lead rope of your friend's horse in your hand. If he decides to break away, drop the rope and I will shoot him."

He nodded his head and took the rope. "I know who you are Señor Taylor. You are well known in this country. They say that you get your man every time, is this true?"

"People tell stories about things they have no knowledge of. I just do my job."

"Are you taking us back to Magdalena?"

"Yes."

"Señor Taylor, the man I took the bulls from lied to me and cheated me out of my wages. He was going to give me three pregnant cows and my wages after one year of work. Instead he told me to get off his land. I had to do something. Can you help me?"

"No, my job is to bring you back, nothing more."

"Do you think they will hang me?"

"Yes. That is what happens with stock thieves."

"Señor, will you tell them that I helped you and did not resist?"

"Yes. They will want to know where the bulls are," said Taylor. "Do you have them?"

"No."

"Where are they?"

"I sold them south to a cousin in Mexico."

*

They rode for several hours through the scruffy, broken desert, winding their way toward the distant mountains. Stopping at a small stream they took a break and watered the horses. Taylor had the Mexican unshackle the big man and re-shackle his hands in front. "Relieve yourself and have some water and jerky. The country gets rougher from here to town." Still pointing his rifle at the big man he motioned for him to sit. "When we move out I will shackle you in front so you can hold on. You know what will happen if you try to escape." Taylor watched the man take a drink then sit down under a cottonwood tree. His Winchester never left the man's chest from the moment they stopped.

The prisoner finished a long pull from the canteen. "Deputy, you and I have been around a long time. One thing we both know, is that on a long ride like this, there will always be that one moment when you drop your guard. When you look away or when your horse shies, I'll be ready."

Taylor shrugged. "The warrant for your arrest says: *recover subject dead or alive.* It is less trouble to bring you back to town over the saddle than in it. You do what you need to do and I will do what I need to do."

Moving slowly through the sage and cactus, the riders began a long steep climb. Cedar and piñon covered the hillsides and the ground was littered with loose, broken rock, cholla cactus and cut through with deep arroyos. For an hour they wound their way in the hot midday sun to the top of a high, flat mesa that ran for several miles. At the end of the mesa, Taylor turned them up a small creek and began to head toward the mountains. The horses picked their way through the water, and the cottonwoods along the bank gave way to ponderosa pines and large groves of aspen trees. They picked up a faint trail beside the creek and it quickly became steeper and more difficult to navigate.

Turning into a sharp uphill curve, the lead horses' foot slipped on a broken rock and the shoe slapped loudly against it. Rearing up, it slid back into the second horse causing it to stumble backward, sliding down the trail in a tangle of horses, reins and rocks. Both outlaws and horses lay in a twisted pile, half in and half out of the creek.

Jumping off his horse, José walked up to the mess. The Mexican was wrapped up tight in the big man's arms. The prisoner squeezed the shackle chain against the old man's neck as the creek swirled around them. "Looks like this is one of those moments deputy." He held the man close to his chest, covering himself almost completely. "Just throw down your rifle and let me get on my horse and I won't kill him."

"I told you what would happen if you tried to escape.

"I don't care what you said, let me go or he dies."

"It does not matter, go ahead and kill him," said Taylor, with his rifle still pointed at him.

"What the hell do you mean it don't matter?"

"Both of you have dead or alive on your warrants. You kill him, I kill you. It does not matter who does the killing.

Squeezing the chain tighter around the Mexican's neck, he leaned his head to the right a few more inches, just enough to clearly see what Taylor was doing.

The .44-40 bullet went through the killers right eye, blowing a bloody spray across the trees and the horses. The gunshot caused the horses to thrash even harder and roll tight against the dead man. Piercing the cantle on one of the saddles, the slug was finally stopped by a tree root.

Rolling over and grabbing his ear, the Mexican was screaming he'd been shot. Taylor pulled his hand back to look at the wound. A small, half-moon shaped hole had cut cleanly through the edge of his ear. "You shot me! I did nothing and you shot me . . !"

"I shot the man who was going to kill you, the ear will heal. Get the horses sorted out and we will load him and head back."

After several more miles they began to descend into a wide sage flat and made their way into town. Tying up in front of the sheriff's office, Taylor led the Mexican to the cell. He laid the paperwork on the sheriff's desk. "The big one is out on the horse. The bull thief gave me no resistance and was helpful in getting the other one here. I told him I would tell you that."

The sheriff nodded. "Duly noted."

José brought in the guns, saddlebags and spurs and laid them on the desk. If there was no family to claim the goods, the county sells them after thirty days. "If nobody wants the rifle, I will buy it."

The prisoner complained that he needed a bandage to stop the bleeding from his ear.

"What happened to his ear?"

"It got in the way when I shot the other one. Do you have any more warrants for me?"

"I do, you want 'em right now?"

"No, I will be back for them in the morning."

*

Taylor paid fifty cents for a sleeping pallet at the Lee Fong laundry. He would take one more warrant in the morning. When he finished it, he would head back to the ranch. He'd been a long time on the trail and was caked in fine grit. He planned on washing up in the creek like usual, but the bathing tubs at Fong's were something new in town and the sheriff recommended he should try it. He paid another fifty cents for a bathing tub with hot water. They also provided a bar of soap and a large towel with the bath.

An older, stoop-shouldered Chinese woman showed him to the bathing area, a room with two wooden tubs and a wood stove for heating the water. One end of the small room had an open doorway, covered only by white canvas and one window. Several large copper pots full of water were already heating on the stove.

Clean clothes were a rare luxury for him and he paid twenty-five cents to have his clothes brushed. A bath in a tub full of hot water would be a new experience for him. He gave the girl another fifteen cents to have his black Stetson brushed and his black stovepipe boots cleaned and polished. His rifle and pistol sat on a chair inches from the tub. He could see why the bathing tub was becoming popular. The hot water helped wash away some of the soreness as well as the trail dirt.

*

When fully dressed in his high-heel boots and black Stetson, his five-foot eight, hundred and fifty-pound frame looked much more impressive. He dressed in a long black duster, black trousers and a black vest over a long sleeve, white shirt buttoned at the collar. He was noted for his dark good looks and black mustache.

Often described as serious and intense and sometimes scary, he had few friends and no wife, just his horses and his small ranch. After the bath, he had a steak and two glasses of beer for supper. He slept well for several hours, waking up just before sunrise. When he finished cleaning his rifle and pistol, he reloaded and made the short walk to the sheriff's office. "I am ready, what do you have for me?"

"Before you leave, the trial for the Mexican that stole the bulls is coming up. They may need you to testify."

"When is it?"

"In three days."

"I will be there."

"Then here's two more," he said, sliding the paperwork across the desk. "One is wanted for forgery of land claims and the other shot a preacher. They say the preacher had eyes for his girl."

"Did he kill him?"

"No, he shot him in the hip. It's not too bad, but he'll be limping for a while. The forger is some guy named Atticus Boggs. Unless he's taken the train out of town already, he won't be too hard to find, he's a city fellow. Just let that one go, we don't need to worry about him right now. The other guy, a cowboy named Hinton, was drunk and blowing off steam when he met up with the preacher. I'd start looking for him at the C bar J outfit. If they ain't hiding him out, someone there likely knows where he's at. Here's the warrant."

*

WANTED:

<u>Walter Hinton:</u> attempted murder.
White - 33 years old - 6' tall – 160 pounds – brown hair
Considered armed and dangerous
Known to work for C bar J Ranch
Deliver subject to Socorro County Jail, Magdalena office

Short, with a bushy gray beard and enormous pot belly, Sheriff Vernon Davis had been a lawman for more than twenty-five years. He'd seen a lot of things in his time on the job, but he had never met anyone like José Taylor. The man lived his life to track down outlaws. The first one he went after was the man who killed his mother. Davis was shorthanded when it happened and against his better judgment, deputized a very young Taylor to look for the killer. A week later he brought him in over the saddle. In the years since, he had brought back more than seventy outlaws, nineteen of them over the saddle. He was well known in the territory as a man not to be trifled with. Davis lit a fresh cigar. "You know there's still Indian Jake . . ."

"Has he been heard from lately?" asked José.

"Word is he was down in Texas a couple of weeks ago. It looks like he stole a few horses outside of Odessa and shot a cowboy in the deal."

"Did he kill him?"

"Not this time. He shot his horse out from under him and hit him in the leg."

"When I get back let me know if you have heard of him in the territory. Then I will bring him in."

Taylor walked through the livery to the pens in back. Three of the horses inside were his, the sorrel he just used, one tall buckskin gelding and a mare that he purchased recently. Choosing the buckskin, he saddled him and tied him up in the alley. "Heading out already?" asked the livery owner.

He nodded. "There are always plenty of outlaws that need catching, that is what I do."

"Do you want me to take these other two mounts out to your place?"

"Yes, thank you. Tell Albert to turn them into the back pasture and that I will be back in a day or two."

"Will do. I heard the other day that old Indian Jake might be in this part of the country; you goin' after him?"

"If he is here, I will go after him."

Chapter 2

José mounted up and headed for the C bar J outfit. Riding slowly up to the main house, the long-time ranch manager, Tom Selby, came out to meet him. "José, what brings you up here?"

"Where is he Tom?"

"Where is who?"

"Your hand, Walter Hinton, I have a warrant on him."

"Aw shit José, he didn't mean nothin' when he shot that preacher. It was just the whisky talkin'. I can't afford to lose a hand right now; we're smack in the middle of our spring works. What if he turns himself in when we're done?"

"Where is he Tom?"

Selby shrugged. "He's up in camp two. You know where that is?"

"I will find it."

He knew Taylor well enough to know nothing would ever deter him from his mission. "Just follow the trail across the long flat, and through the big stand of quakies. about five miles or so."

Taylor could hear the bawling cattle as he rode into the aspen trees and climbed off his horse. Looking through the trees he could see the cowboys working the cattle. One end of the meadow was a temporary pen full of cows and calves. Two cowboys on horseback roped the calves by the heels and drug them to one of the branding fires. Several irons glowed in the coals where other ranch hands pinned the calves to the ground and put the hot iron to the flank. The men cut the bull calves, notched their ears and turned them loose for their mothers to find.

A thin haze of wood smoke and the unmistakable smell of burning hair drifted through the trees and Taylor watched for a moment until he found his man. Mounted on a tall gray, the cowboy expertly caught a calf, dallied up and spurred his horse, dragging the bawling calf to the fire. When it was hit with the hot iron, they were momentarily engulfed in thick acrid smoke. Choosing this moment to step out of the trees, he walked straight to the mounted cowboy with his Winchester pointed at him. "Walter Hinton, get off the horse."

The cowboy looked down at the man standing in front of him. Taylor's large black Stetson rested just above his eyes and he stared down the long barrel of the rifle pointed at the cowboy's chest.

"Who the hell are you?"

"I am Deputy Sheriff José Taylor. I am here to take you in for attempted murder — get down now."

"You really think you can take me in, little man?"

Get down now or I will shoot you."

Staring at the man with the rifle, the cowboy appeared to be weighing his options. "Walt — don't do it," said one of the cowboys at the fire. "Do you know who he is?"

"I could care less who he is, he ain't takin' me nowhere."

The rest of the cowboys slowly began to move away from the fire. "Walt—this is José Taylor. He hunts down the worst criminals in the territory. He usually brings them back over the saddle. Don't be stupid, just get down."

Taylor remained motionless; the Winchester still pointed at the man's chest. The cowboy stared into Taylor's dark eyes for a long moment. "Okay, I'm gettin' down. Don't do no shootin'."

Taylor gave his shackles to the cowboy that did the talking. "Put these on him in the front and put a halter with a long rope on his horse." After he mounted up, José tied his hands to the saddle. "If he has any personal possessions or pay coming, tell Tom to bring them to the jail. The horse will be at the livery."

"Deputy, I ain't a bad man, I was just drunk is all."

13

"I do not care." Spurring his horse they disappeared through the trees.

A wire from the silver city sheriff confirmed that Atticus Boggs was in their jail. He was in trouble for trying to scam a local out of his money on a land sale. "He will be in there for a while," said Davis. "No need to hurry down there right now. We'll bring him back when they're through with him. You wantin' to go back out right away?"

Jose' shook his head. "I am heading to the ranch. I have a couple of new horses to work."

Davis nodded. "If something comes up I'll let you know. The trial of the bull thief is Tuesday at 10:00 a.m. I'll see you then. Oh yeah, take this rifle you wanted. I'll take five dollars out of your pay."

The ranch was an hour's ride west of town and he hadn't been home in a week. Riding into the barn he stopped at the water trough. Throwing the reins over the fence, he let his horse drink while he took off the saddle. Hanging his hat on a peg, he splashed a little water on his hands and face.

"Hello boss, home for a while?"

"Hello Albert, maybe a few days. How are the horses?"

"All are pretty good. The older black gelding might have something going on with his left hind foot. He didn't want me anywhere near him yesterday when I tried to check it. He's just out back."

Albert and Laura Green had been with him for nearly ten years. Both came from families that were slaves on rice and cotton plantations in North Carolina and Georgia. He met them when he bought the ranch. Albert had been a horseman all his life and José offered him and his wife a job immediately. He took care of the ranch and the horses and Laura took care of the house and the cooking. They lived in the main house with him. "Albert, turn this one into the back pasture and run that gelding in here. I want to take a look at that foot."

Horses were Taylor's singular love in life. He raised them, broke them, doctored them and cared for them as though they were his own children. Twenty-five at last count; he knew each one by name and disposition, keeping a detailed log of their history. As Albert led the gelding into the barn, José watched his gait and the way he favored his hind foot.

"Tell Isaac to come here and ask Laura to make us some supper please. I'll take care of this." Snubbing the gelding off on the gate, he combed and brushed him while he talked to him and fed him a few oats. Rubbing his ears, the horse responded with a gentle nuzzle. Within a few minutes he had the leg up and was looking at a large piece of rock wedged inside the shoe pressing up into the foot. Prying out the rock he could feel the horse relax and finished cleaning up the hoof. Feeding him a few more oats, he led him to the small pen where he could watch him move. If everything looked good, he would turn him into the big pasture after supper.

Isaac had worked for José for a year, and had become a loyal worker and excellent horseman. A nephew of Albert's from someplace in the South, José hired him on his recommendation. Tall and lean, he had powerful arms and shoulders and could easily out work any two men. He had become part of the family and lived in a small cabin behind the main house.

"Hey boss, how was your trip?"

"It was good. Isaac, do you have a rifle?"

"No sir, I never had a rifle of my own before, but I have used one back home, on turkeys and deer and such."

José handed him the rifle he bought from the sheriff and a box of cartridges. "I would like you to learn to shoot this one. Will that be okay with you?"

"Yessir, that would be good by me."

"Good. Tomorrow we will have a shooting lesson."

Chapter 3

After three days, he was ready to go back to work. The remuda looked good and the ranch was running well. Isaac proved to be good with the rifle and José was glad to have someone else on the ranch with good shooting skills. The ranch was in a remote part of the county and you never knew what might happen.

Picking a young bay with two white socks, he headed for town. The trial of the Mexican bull thief had just started when he

16

walked into the small makeshift courtroom in the schoolhouse. After ten minutes of testimony from the rancher, the judge asked the Mexican if he had anything to say in his defense.

"Si, your honor, I do. This man did not pay me as promised after working for him. He told me that if I would work for one year on his ranch for a bed in the bunkhouse and meals, at the end he would give me three pregnant cows and my wages. Instead, after a year he just told me to leave his land."

"Did you steal his bulls?"

"Si, I took them. I had to have something for my work."

"You knew it was illegal to steal them?"

"Si, I knew."

"Where are the bulls now?"

"I sold them down in Mexico."

"Okay, the jury will deliberate now," said the judge, banging his gavel. When the jury left the room the judge, a huge round man easily over four-hundred pounds stood up and went to his office. Judge Myron Coker was known to be cold and indifferent to the defendants in his court. Some days he ate and drank while on the bench and was known to fall asleep in the middle of a long trial. His judgments were always inconsistent.

Twenty minutes later the jury filed in and the judge returned with a bottle in one hand and his gavel in the other. "What say you on the matter of the stolen bulls?"

Before the jury could read the verdict, the defendant stood up and pleaded for mercy. "Please, I did not resist, and I helped the deputy get the other man back to the jail, he can tell you."

"Deputy Taylor, do you have anything to add to this proceeding?"

Jośe nodded. "It is as he said. He did not resist and he was helpful in getting the other outlaw back to town."

"Please read the verdict now," said the judge.

"We find the defendant guilty of two counts of stock theft."

The judge nodded. "Very well. The defendant shall be hanged by the neck until dead, one week from today." As the sheriff led the Mexican down the aisle he looked at Jośe.

"Please, señor, can you help me?"

Jośe shook his head."

At the jail, the sheriff handed Jośe a poster with a picture and a description of the wanted man. "This one is a killer and a coward. Him and another man kidnapped a young Navajo woman from the Ramah Reservation and are thought to be holed up somewhere up in the Zuni Mountains. The Indians are threatening retaliation if she's not returned. We need it done by a legal deputy of the law so the rest of the tribal members are satisfied that they are treated fairly."

"That is up in Cibola County, it may take me a little longer to get it done."

"Your jurisdiction is the whole of the New Mexico Territory. The local sheriff hasn't had any luck catching up to them and asked if you could help. If you need anything, stop at the reservation and introduce yourself. Bring the men to their jail and they will handle everything from there."

"I will not need anything."

"Here are the warrants. He's also suspected in two other murders. Be careful, this guy seems to like killing."

"I will wire you when I finish." José sat on his heels, warming his hands over the fire. After three days of travel he was camped on the south side of the Zuni Mountains. Looking at the warrants, he went over the details again.

*

WANTED:

__Royal Morton:__ – murder – kidnapping – larceny
– horse theft.
White - 40 years old – 5' 9" – 160 pounds – brown
hair – scar on left forearm
Known to be heavily armed and extremely
dangerous
Recover subject dead or alive.
Deliver subject to Ramah Navajo Reservation

__Virgil Henry:__ kidnapping – cattle and horse theft – trespass
White - 51 years old – 5' 11" – 190 pounds – red
hair – scar on right side of chin
Considered armed and dangerous
Recover subject dead or alive
Deliver subject to Ramah Navajo Reservation

The paperwork said the two white men had kidnapped a young Navajo girl while she was gathering firewood near the reservation. Several ranchers had already seen and identified the two as being in the area, and several Navajo men had reported running them off the reservation a couple days before. By the time the local law had arrived, they were long gone. He folded up the papers and returned them to his saddle bag.

He'd been in the Zuni Mountains several times over the years and had a pretty good feel for the lay of the land. He started his search in the foothills east of the reservation. Following a wide canyon, he worked his way up onto a barren mesa covered in sage and into the low foothills of the mountains. This was historically sheep country and remote camps were scattered all over the hills, most of them abandoned over the years.

He knew the outlaws would need the same things most animals did, water and food. Food could be found easy enough for a man with a rifle, but water could be difficult in country as dry as this. He methodically rode the foothills checking every drainage for any sign of water. This time of year, most water would be from one of the small springs that were scattered through the mountains. For several days he covered the south side of the mountains finding several springs and more abandoned sheep camps.

He camped each night near one of the springs providing water and just enough grass for his horse. Every night he slept without a fire, not wanting to give away his position to anyone in the area.

Each day he woke before sunup and climbed to a high point looking for a sign of a fire or someone in the area. Every day the sun was relentlessly hot without a cloud in sight. He crossed over the mountains through a cut so narrow he had to lead the horse on foot.

Leaving the canyon, the view opened up to a steep game trail winding down the mountainside. Finding a wide flat spot, partway down the mountain with a tiny, nearly invisible spring and good patch of wet grass, he decided to camp there for the night.

After a week on the trail his food supply was down to a handful of dried venison and two apples. He couldn't fire his rifle and take a chance that his quarry might hear him. He had used a snare twice already to trap rabbits, eating the meat raw. If he didn't find some sign tomorrow, he would have to kill something or go to the reservation for supplies.

Waking up well before sunup he walked through the last of the moonlight to a high piece of rimrock and waited. Just as the sun began to rise he noticed a faint smell of wood smoke. It made its way up the valley as the sun warmed the air. He scanned the miles of trees below him with his binoculars until he found the source. A thin swirl of white smoke hung above a long narrow meadow. He could see a sliver of water running through the middle of it. *A perfect place for sheep*, he thought. *And maybe a perfect place for outlaws too.*

Leading his horse down through the cedars he tied it up short of the clearing. Checking his rifle and pistol, he made his way through the trees to the edge of the opening. Backed up against the trees was a small square log cabin with one end built into the side hill and covered with a sod roof. A rusty tin stove pipe stood several feet above the roofline leaning hard toward the back and the smoke swirled lazily uphill. Two horses in hobbles were feeding in the grass below the cabin.

As he took in the scene a woman stepped out the door and picked up several pieces of firewood. Barefoot, wearing long black braids and a buckskin dress, he knew that he'd found the missing Navajo girl. Half a deer carcass hung in a tree near the cabin and water seeped out of a spring through a crack in a rock face next to it. He decided to watch for a while and see if the two men would come out.

When the sun got higher, the taller man came out. He was bare-chested except for suspenders, and walked straight into the trees and out of sight. Taking advantage of the moment, José quietly fell in a few steps behind him. A hundred yards into the trees, the man dropped his trousers and relieved himself. Standing up, he began to button up. José stepped up and pressed the muzzle of the rifle to the back of his head. "Be very quiet and do what I say or I will kill you."

"Who the hell are you?"

"Put your hands up so I can see them."

His hands went up quickly. "They're up, now who are you and what do you want?"

"I am Deputy Sheriff José Taylor. I am here to take you and your partner to jail."

"You think that you can get that done? My partner is a dead shot, if you try and take him you'll be damn sorry you ever tried."

"Put your hands down and lean back against that quakie."

He leaned against the tree and José pulled his hands behind it, clicking the shackles on his wrists.

"You can't leave me hitched up to this tree! Goddamn you anyway you son-of-a-bitch — when I get out . . ."

Before he could say anything else, the butt of the Winchester caught him on the jaw hard enough to knock him out. José watched as he slid down the trunk of the tree. Moving to the cabin door he listened as the man inside gave the woman orders. "Cut off a piece of that buck and get it on the skillet — I'm starving." Grabbing the knife, the woman started toward the door. "And find that idiot partner and tell him to bring some water when he comes back."

Stepping through the door, she turned to close it and came eye to eye with José. He had his rifle pointed directly at her and his finger across his lips to shush her. She nodded and closed the door. He pointed to the trees and she understood instantly to move away from the cabin. Looking through a crack in the door, he could see the man with the scar on his left forearm sitting on the makeshift pallet. A revolver lay on the table and a rifle was next to him, inches from his hand.

He stood to one side of the door and knocked on it. "What the hell is your problem? Just open the goddamn door!"

José knocked again, and stepped back several feet. The door flew open, hit the cabin wall and bounced back at the outlaw. When the man put one hand out to stop it he saw the Winchester was leveled at his heart. "I am Deputy Sheriff José Taylor and you are under arrest."

The cowboy stood staring at him, his rifle in one hand, not believing what he was seeing. "How the hell did you find me?"

"Drop your rifle and put your hands up."

"Or what little man? You gonna shoot me?"

"Yes."

Spinning around, the man dove into the cabin and ended up on his back firing his rifle through the door. As it slammed shut, José saw the Indian woman dart from the trees and climb onto the sod roof. She kicked the crooked stove pipe over, causing the lower section to fall inside.

Jumping down from the roof she looked at him. "He will come out soon."

Within minutes, the door flew open again and the outlaw came out in a rush of wood smoke shooting wildly, but he couldn't see his target well enough to hit it. José put one bullet in his chest and it was over.

"Where is the other man?" asked the woman.

"I have him up in the trees. You wait here and I will get him. What is your name?"

"I am Sara Song, from the Ramah Navajo Reservation."

He looked at the dirty figure in front of him. She was small, with long hair braided in back, a filthy deerskin dress and no moccasin's. He could see that she was very pretty, even through the dirt.

"I am Deputy Sheriff José Taylor."

"You will bring the other man now?"

He nodded. "I will get him. Gather up the horses and whatever items you want and we will go."

Unhooking his prisoner from the tree, he put the shackles on behind him and walked him to the cabin. The Indian woman had the two horses of the outlaws waiting and had found José's and brought it to the cabin.

Sitting the prisoner on the ground, he rolled the dead man over and started to tie his ankles together. The woman walked by him quickly, heading straight for the prisoner. After saying something to the man that he didn't understand, she pulled out a long butcher knife and buried it in the middle of his chest, all the way to the hilt. Pulling it out quickly, blood pumped from the wound in small spurts. She plunged it in again and again. He watched as she dealt her revenge to her tormenter.

She dropped the knife and walked around the body several times, cursing the dead man, kicking dirt on him and finally spitting on him. She had taken her revenge and was ready to move on. "Are we ready to leave, Mister José Taylor?"

Nothing ever shocked him, but this was the first time he'd seen anything like this. "Yes, we are ready to go. You will have to ride behind me — and throw that knife in the fire."

"That will be okay."

Tying the two dead outlaws on their horses, they started the long ride back to the reservation and they took it slow, camping one night on the south side of the mountains. She started a fire and put a piece of deer meat on a spit. "What are you going to do with me? Are you going to take me for your own?"

He was surprised at this curious question. "Why do you think that? Your tribal police asked that we return you to the reservation, that is why I am here."

"There is nothing for me back there. I live alone and have no family and no man. If I return now, they will consider me dirty and shun me even worse."

"This is not your fault," said José. "I will tell them that you were brave and unafraid of these men."

"It will not matter to them; they will not want me."

He shrugged. "We need to sleep now; we have a long ride tomorrow." After loading the two dead men, he mounted his horse and she climbed up behind him and they headed for the reservation. Neither spoke for an hour.

Finally, she tapped him on the shoulder. "Mister José, I am a very good cook, the medicine man's wife taught me well."

In a few more miles, she tapped him on the shoulder again.

"Mister José, I keep a very clean hogan."

26

A few miles farther she tapped him on the shoulder a third time, leaning very close to his ear. "Mister José, I know how to take care of horses and sheep and cows and goats."

They rode into the reservation and she jumped down, took the lead rope and walked the horses with the dead outlaws to the tribal police station. "Come out Robert, and take these pieces of garbage from me."

The police chief stepped outside the door and looked at the two dead men. "Sara Song, I did not think I would see you alive again. I thought someone would find your dead body."

"Robert Nahabe, you are a useless old man. You could have come after me, but you didn't. You are a shame to our people."

"Maybe you weren't worth going after . . ."

Dropping the ropes, she charged the old man with her fists flying, raining blows on his head as fast as she could. The chief pushed her to the ground and she was up and back on him in an instant. After hitting the ground a third time, José stepped in between them and grabbed her by the wrist.

"She hit a police officer, she has to answer for this to the tribal court," said Nahabe. "She's coming with me."

"No," said José, "she is coming with me."

"With you? Just who do you think you are? You are on Navajo land and she will do what I say."

"I am Deputy Sheriff José Taylor. I have warrants for both these men and orders to drop them off with you. My job is done."

The chief had heard stories about this man before but this was their first meeting. "Okay, you can go, she is nothing but a problem to everyone here."

Still holding her, he asked where her hogan was. "It is close, this way . . ."

With the reins of his horse in one hand and her wrist in the other they walked to the hogan.

"Are you going to let me go?"

"I will let you go, if you go inside right now."

"I will go in."

The hogan was a small, round room with a wood frame covered in branches and mud on the top. A battered, tin sheepherder's stove was used for cooking and heat. The room was nearly empty except for a sleeping pallet, two baskets with blankets and clothes and a cooking pot.

"The whores! The dirty dog whores have taken my skillet and my knife — I will find them and they will pay!"

He stopped her before she could get out the door. "Stop and listen — now!"

"What? They cannot take my things like that."

"Stop."

"Why?"

"You asked me if I was going to take you for my own."

"So?"

"Do you want to be with me?"

"You want me?"

"That is what I asked."

She looked into his eyes, hardly able to believe what she had just heard. She touched his face with both hands, running her fingers across his lips. "Mister José Taylor, this mouth had better be truthful. I will not be with a man who lies to me."

"I do not lie."

"You saw me kill a man and you still want me?"

"I want you to be with me."

She nodded, "I will be with you Mister José Taylor. Where will we go?"

"We will go to my ranch, south of here near a town called Magdalena."

She thought about this for a minute. "I think that would be good, but we must be married first. I will go and find the medicine man. When I return, we will become husband and wife."

When she left the hogan he sat on the pallet wondering what just happened. What was it about this woman that had made him act so impulsively — something so totally out of character for him? He'd never been with a woman before, and he'd never met a woman such as this before.

His heart was racing, his hands shook and his face felt flush. All these feelings were new to him. He did not know what was happening, but he knew for certain he wanted to be with her. For the first time in his life he was not in control of the situation, and he was not quite sure what to do about it.

He had thought about a Christian minister in Magdalena to marry them, but if she wanted to do it this way, it was okay with him. This scrappy little Indian woman was a match for anyone, no matter if it's a man or woman or what their size may be. He didn't understand what he was experiencing, but somehow he knew it was the right thing.

She walked back into the hogan with a short, heavy Indian man and his wife, a woman nearly as small as her carrying a large basket. "You men go outside now and come back in a while," said the medicine man's wife, shooing them out the door. "And bring the water when you return."

Standing in front of the hogan with the medicine man, he wondered what he should do next. "Young man, walk with me while we talk. Sara Song is a special woman, but I think you know this already."

"I do. But can you tell me why she is alone? Why does she think she is an outcast in the Navajo Nation?"

The medicine man stopped walking for a moment. "Her parents and her brothers were killed by white outlaws when she was very little. A family here took her in and raised her for a few years, then they all died from smallpox except her. After that, my wife and I took her in. When she was with us, our new baby daughter died. She is much smarter than most men or women and can work any man to exhaustion. She is like a daughter to us, like the one we lost.

Her second family was known for their good horses and she became very good at riding and training them. But some will say she is bad medicine, and I think she has begun to believe it. We helped her build her own hogan and she has been alone since then."

"Those things were not her fault," said José.

"These are just the beliefs of our people. Who am I to say different? Our tradition says that once married, the daughter and her husband will go to live with her parents in their hogan. She has no family so that cannot happen. You will have to make a home for her."

Stopping at his hogan, the medicine man came out with an unusual looking jug with two spouts. José had never seen one like it before. "Why does it have two spouts?"

"It is for the wedding, you will see. This will be a small ceremony as my wife and I are the only guests. We should go back to the lodge now."

"I must stop and see the police chief first, then I will be there."

José walked into to the chief's office. "I would like to buy one of the horses I brought in."

"Why? They're nothing special."

"I will give you ten dollars for the bay."

"Fifteen dollars and you must take both of them."

"I will pay fifteen dollars for both with the saddles and bridles, and the colt pistol."

The police chief pulled the gun out of the drawer and looked it over. "Twenty for everything or no deal."

He reached into his pocket and pulled out a twenty-dollar gold coin and dropped it on the desk. "You saddle them and have them in front in an hour." Picking up the pistol he walked out the door and headed for his wedding.

When he returned to the hogan, his bride was standing between the medicine man and his wife. Dressed in a white, fringed buckskin dress and a red, waist length coat covered with elk teeth, she was the most beautiful woman he had ever seen. Her hair hung straight down in braids, nearly to her waist. A headpiece made of white and blue beads and red beaded earrings made him think of his mother for the first time in a long while. He wished she could be here to see what a beautiful woman he was about to marry.

The medicine man moved them all together in a circle and handed him a round, flat basket with blue cornmeal mush in it. "Eat, then pass it around." After they all had a portion, he handed him the jar with two spouts. "Each of you drink from one side. Sara Song, you are first, then give the other side to your young man."

After they drank separately they both drank together, as the medicine man, a Hataali, (singer) spoke some words to them in Navajo. He then performed a traditional song and placed their hands together. "You are now joined as husband and wife. May you have a good life together."

She kissed her new husband and hugged the medicine man and his wife. After speaking in Navajo with them for a few minutes, they left the hogan. "Husband, will we stay here tonight?"

"No. I have purchased the horses of the outlaws and want to start out on the trail."

José and Sara Song packed the extra horse with her possessions and covered everything with a buffalo robe. Riding out of the reservation, she never looked back.

Chapter 4

As the sun got low, José pulled off the trail and into a wide grassy meadow. A small stream wandered through the thick grass, disappearing into the trees. He tied the three horses to a long picket line. Just above the water, Sara Song spread two buffalo robes on the grass and built a fire next to them. Preparing a meal of dried goat meat and fried bread with currents and chokecherries, she dropped the bread in the skillet just as he walked up.

I thought you did not have a skillet anymore?"

"I could not let someone steal from me. Before the ceremony I found the one who stole my knife and skillet and took them back. Sit down husband and we shall eat."

They ate slowly, just as the sun was setting. After the meal, she added wood to the fire and sat down on the robes. They lay back on the robe looking up at the stars. "The medicine man told you why I was alone?"

"Yes. He said people think you are bad medicine, what we call a jinx."

"Do you believe I am bad medicine?"

"No, I believe you are good medicine. How else could a man such as myself ever find so beautiful a woman to be his wife?"

"Husband, I think your eyes are clouded. No man has called me beautiful before."

"My eyes are clear. The others are not able to see through their superstitions. We will have a wonderful life together, and we will have handsome baby boys and beautiful baby girls."

Tears started down her cheeks and she looked at him, kissing him gently and running her fingers through his thick hair. "Remember, you said you would never lie to me . . ."

"I will never lie to you, that is my promise." He pulled her close.

"Will you also promise never to hurt me?"

Wrapping her in his arms he whispered to her, "I will never hurt you and I will never let anyone else hurt you."

She began to cry softly against his chest. "Thank you for taking me for your own." They lay back on the robes cradled in each other's arms and fell asleep. They woke up still wrapped together, listening to the sound of coyotes singing all around them.

The embers of the fire glowed against the night sky and they covered up with the robe and made love for the first time.

When he woke up in the morning he was alone on the robes. Looking around, he saw there was a new fire laid in and a freshly cleaned rabbit next to it. The picket rope had been moved and the horses were on fresh grass.

He saw his bride, standing in the soft morning light, knee deep in the stream washing herself. He lay back on the robes and watched his beautiful new wife walk back to the camp. "Is it your custom to walk around without clothes?"

"There is no one here to see me but the coyote's and the birds, and you have already seen me."

Standing in the morning light he could see how truly beautiful she was. Her long black hair, now dripping wet without braids, hung down across her breasts nearly reaching her waist. He could also see several fading bruises on her arms, evidence of her captors' violence. She picked up her dress and dropped it over her head, letting it fall to her knees and slipped on her moccasins. After wrapping a red cloth belt around her waist, she pushed her knife and sheath into it.

"Husband, am I still beautiful to you?"

"You are even more beautiful this morning."

"You must tell me each day that I am beautiful . . ."

"That will be easy. How did you get the rabbit this morning?"

"I hit it with a rock."

"Good, I like rabbit."

"Rest on the robes, it will be ready soon."

"After I have my meal, may I have you?"

It took her a moment to understand what he meant. When it came to her what he was saying, she broke into a smile.

"Maybe — if you treat me right . . ."

*

José and Sara Song rode into the ranch, stopping at the barn. Albert took the reins and tied up the horses. "This is my wife Sara Song, she is from the Ramah Navajo Reservation. Albert is the ranch manager and his wife Laura takes care of everything inside the cabin."

She stared at the man for a moment. She hadn't seen many black men, particularly one as dark as this. "Hello Albert. I will help you with the horses . . ."

"It's okay Missy, I'll do it. You and the boss go ahead to the house and meet Laura and I will be along shortly."

He introduced her to Laura and Isaac. "This is my wife, Sara Song. She is the new Missus of the Taylor house. Isaac works with Albert around the ranch. He lives in the cabin out back, but he joins us for the evening meal." Isaac was tall and slim, with much lighter skin than Albert and Laura. He had handsome features and a broad smile.

"Albert and Laura have a sleeping room in back and this one is mine." He walked into the room and sat with her on the bed. "This is our room now. You may do anything to it you would like.

Laura and Albert and Isaac are here to help you with anything you need."

The room was nearly empty of anything but the bed, a coat hanging on the wall and a few clothes on a small table. The single window had no covering and the glass was cracked. "Husband, I will need to work too, what can I do in this beautiful hogan?"

"You can do as much or as little as you want." Walking through the house, she took in every detail, noting where everything was. The kitchen was a small area added on to the original cabin and Albert and Laura's sleeping room was next to it. There was a large four hole cook stove and a hand-operated pitcher pump to bring water into the house. These were all new to her. A fireplace in their sleeping room and a larger one in the main room were for heat.

"Husband, I never saw a hogan so large for so few people."

He put his arm around her and squeezed tightly. "Then we must fill it up with so many babies there will be no more room."

"After a few days, she was comfortable in the ranch house and quickly became close to Laura. Albert, a quiet man by nature, took a little longer to know. One day he asked her if she would like to choose a horse for herself.

"A horse of my own? I would like that very much. Can we do it now?"

Albert nodded. "Meet me at the barn in a few minutes and we will look them over."

Standing at the fence, they watched as Isaac moved several young horses into the pen. "These are almost ready to ride. If you pick one out, Isaac can have it ready in a few weeks."

As the horses walked around in the pen, one reared up for a moment then walked straight to her and hung her head over the fence. "I think she likes me, and I think I like her." She rubbed her ears and ran her fingers through her mane. "Yes, this is the one."

Albert pointed at the beautiful black and white mare for Isaac to cut out and take to the smaller pen. Until now, this had been a very standoffish and wild horse. They had been working with the young horses for a while, but this one was always more difficult to catch. Albert had never seen her come to anyone before.

Returning from town, José tied his horse to the fence next to Albert. "That's the one she wants?"

"She came right to her at the fence. I think there is some kind of connection there."

"Okay, let me know when she is ready."

Laura and Sara Song quickly formed a close friendship. They shared work around the house and cleaning was something they both liked and worked hard at. They spent long hours together in the kitchen teaching each other different meals.

"Albert, I do believe you and I are getting fat from all this good cooking," said José at supper one night.

"We can stop cooking if you want," said Sara Song. "Soon you will look like a skinny old reservation dog."

"No," said José. "We would not want to change anything, would we Albert?"

"No sir, don't want no change here."

She bent down and kissed him on the cheek. "A fat husband is okay with me. He will keep me warmer at night." She took over the job of keeping the firewood stocked, and tending the garden as well as sharing the household work. For the first time in her life she felt like she had a real family and a real home. She also liked that she was now Sara Song Taylor, wife of Deputy Sheriff José Taylor.

When her horse was ready, José and Albert watched her walk into the pen and untie the reins. Pulling herself into the saddle she walked the horse slowly around the pen several times. Looking at Isaac, she pointed at the gate. When they cleared the pen, she slapped her with the reins and the mare took off on a dead run. They ran flat out to the far side of the ranch and circled back never breaking stride. When they got back to the pen, she slid to a stop, jumped off and tied her to the rail. José and Albert realized that she never had her feet in the stirrups the whole time.

"Wife, you did not have your feet in the stirrups, why is that?"

"I had no saddle on the reservation, I will get used to it in a while. This is a wonderful horse; I will call her Fast Wind." She rubbed her ears and chin and the horse nuzzled her back. "We will be great friends forever, thank you husband."

Chapter 5

José gave Albert a few last-minute instructions about the horses. "I will be gone for a few days; I have a suspect to pick up down near Ruidoso." He hugged Sara Song, kissed her on the cheek and headed for town.

Sheriff Davis handed him a poster and a warrant for a man named Pierce Miller, an army deserter turned horse thief and outlaw. "Drop this one off at Fort Stanton, the army wants him first." He looked at the poster and read the warrant.

*

WANTED:

Pierce Miller: Desertion from U.S. Army, horse theft and robbery
White, 44 years old, 5'-10" tall, 185 lbs.
Considered armed and dangerous .
Return subject to Fort Stanton Military Reservation.

*

"I will find him. Have you heard any more about Indian Jake?"

"I just heard that he might be up in the Raton area. I'm waiting for the sheriff up there to notify me about any sightings."

"What happened with the trial for Walter Hinton — the one who shot the preacher."

"Judge Coker fined him twenty dollars, released him and told him to go back to work. He told the preacher he shouldn't mess around with another man's woman and that he's lucky Walter Hinton didn't kill him."

"Twenty dollars for shooting someone?" said José.

"The money was just paid for the judge's trip to town," said Davis. "Otherwise there wouldn't have been any fine."

"Okay. If you hear anything about the Indian, you can leave a wire for me at the fort. I'll check in there when I'm done."

Loading his horse on the train, he would ride all the way to Socorro. It will be easier on his horse and he could get a little sleep on the way. Picking up a few supplies at the local dry goods, he rode the short distance to the Rio Grande and forded it easily. He continued south for a few miles to the village of San Antonio and turned east into the desert. The next leg of his trip would be miles of dry, open country. The heat was intense and he took it slow, often walking his horse or resting until the sun got low.

After the first day on the trail, he found a small stream and camped for the night. For the next two nights, he stopped at any source of water he could find. One night he spotted the tops of several cottonwoods in the distance growing around a marshy pond and another night he camped at a nearly invisible spring in the bottom of an arroyo.

The fourth morning he rode into the badlands, or the *malpais,* as the Mexicans called the ancient lava field. Travel through miles of it was brutal going for horses and men alike. Razor sharp rock and cactus covered the ground for miles in every direction. A good trail through the rock was hard to find. Brutal heat and fine dust blew steadily across the rocks. Everything that could hurt a horse or a man was waiting in the ancient lava field. He rode slowly along the edge of the lava until he came to an opening. After a few minutes, he could see that it was a dead end. He went back to the edge of the black rock and looked for another opening. On the third try he found a path that looked like it could work.

Picking his way slowly along a narrow, wandering trail just wide enough for a horse, he navigated four miles of the unforgiving terrain until he came out on the flat desert ground again. Another day's ride, took him into the northern foothills of the Ruidoso Mountains.

Stopping at a sheepherder's cabin, he tied up and walked toward the Mexican man tending his flock. After a few minutes of conversation in Spanish, the man agreed to let him stay for the night. After taking care of his horse, he brought some dried elk meat into the cabin for supper.

"Señor, have you seen this man?" asked José, showing him the poster with the drawing of Miller.

"No, I have not seen anyone like that. But strangers do not often stop here. If he is hiding in these mountains, I would look farther up into the canyons. There is better water and grass, and more places to hide."

The next morning he thanked the man and handed him a few coins. "Gracias señor."

He spent the next two days checking old sheep camps and isolated canyons looking for any sign of the outlaw. On the second day, he found another sheepherder's camp with a small flock in the meadow. Riding toward him, the herder noticed his badge and waved him over. "I need help please. A man has killed one of my best rams. You are a lawman; can you find him and make him pay me?"

He could see the blood on the ground where the sheep was killed. "What did this man look like?"

"A tall white man leading three horses. He just killed my ram and threw him on a horse and rode away, like I wasn't even here."

"When did he do this?"

"Yesterday, just after the sun came up. He headed down this canyon to the east." The man pointed the way.

He showed him the wanted poster. "Does he look like this?"

"Si, Señor, very much like this."

He knew that trailing this man would be relatively easy, four horses left a lot of sign. "I will let you know what I find when I come back through."

"Muchas gracias, please find this man . . ."

Moving slowly, he would ride a little then stop and look ahead for any sign that he was getting close. For the better part of a day he moved slowly and quietly, looking for any sign of a camp or horses. He stopped for the night, sleeping without a fire and eating a few bites of dried elk and hard biscuits.

The next morning, he followed the canyon as it widened and dropped down into low rolling hills covered with juniper and piñon trees and sagebrush. The tracks led to a small ranch in the valley. He was met by an older white man with a stringy gray beard and a Mexican woman at his side.

"Hola, señor. What can I do for you?"

"Hola. I am looking for a man trailing three horses. Did you see such a man?"

"Si, the horses are here."

"He left them?"

The old man nodded and pointed out back. "Sí. He said that he was going to leave them here and that I was to care for them until he got back. He said he would pay me when he returned."

José climbed into the pen and checked out all three. "These horses are in poor condition; they need time to recover. Are you able to care for them for a while longer?"

"Sí, I know about horses, but most of my feed is for our animals, I will need more."

José handed him several coins. "Take this and buy what you need and I will be back in a few days to get them."

"This is more than enough, Señor Taylor . . ."

"Use it as you need. How is it you know me?"

"Many people know you . . . You are the Mexican lawman that dresses in black and carries a long rifle. You are quite famous to the Mexican people."

"What is your name?"

"I am Franklin, and this is my wife Maria."

"I am José. Thank you and your wife for your help. I will be back after I find the man that stole them."

*

Following the canyon road as it wandered south, he connected to a well-travelled stage road. He rode into Ruidoso, tying up at the local livery. "What is the best place for a room and a meal?"

The young boy, a local Indian , led his horse into a stall. "I've heard the Lincoln House is good sir, but I have never been inside before."

"Have you seen a man come in recently that looks like this?" he asked, holding out the poster. "He would have rode in alone in the last day or two."

"No sir, I do not remember anyone like that. There is another livery south of town, they may have seen him."

"Thank you. Take good care of my horse. I will see you in the morning."

After the man led his horse away, he walked to the local sheriff's office and introduced himself. The long narrow room was part of an adobe building that contained a local cantina. The smell of chilies filled the room. "Sheriff, I am looking for a man named Pierce Miller, an army deserter and outlaw, I have to deliver him to Fort Stanton." He showed him the poster and warrant for his arrest.

The sheriff shook his head. "Haven't seen or heard of anyone like that. You outta Socorro?"

45

"Magdalena, but I work all over the territory."

"Well, good luck. I imagine you'll want to bunk up at the Lincoln House for tonight. Tell them I sent you over, they'll do you right on the bill, I send them a lot of customers."

*

The hotel was named after the president, but was a long way from being beautiful. Ringing the bell on the counter, he scanned the lobby. A long, well-worn bar had a tired looking bison head hanging over the back wall and a painting of President Lincoln under it. Faded red, white and blue bunting hung down either side of the painting. Several men leaned into the bar, drinking and talking loudly about horses. Two women in long dresses were leaning in between them, and a thin cloud of cigar smoke hung from the ceiling.

"Sir, can I help you . . ?"

He turned to see a middle aged Mexican woman looking at him. "Yes, please. A room for the night. Do you serve supper here?"

"We have steak, potatoes and a beer for a dollar and a quarter. We start serving in about an hour."

"That would be good, I will be down in an hour, please reserve one for me."

"It is first come, first served Señor, we have twenty-five steaks today. When the cowboys get here there won't be many left."

"I will be here, thank you."

"I will bring you fresh water and a towel, there is a bar of soap in the room."

Pouring the water into the basin he splashed it on his face and his hair. After he shaved, he laid his rifle on the bed and threw the blanket over it. Checking the Colt, he headed down for supper. The room started to fill up with cowboys.

Taking a seat at a table near the end of the bar, the same Mexican woman came over to him with a beer. "You are lucky, you are steak number twenty-two, as I said, they go fast. How would you like it?"

"Burned."

"Would you like a woman tonight too?"

"No, I would not."

Looking around the room, studying the men in the bar, he wondered if one of them could be his deserter. Not finding a likely suspect, he finished his meal and washed it down with a second beer. As he got ready to leave, one of the cowboys at the bar came over and sat across from him. Pulling off his hat, he wiped at the brim with his sleeve. "You the law?"

"I am."

"I heard you're lookin' for an army deserter who steals horses, that right?"

He nodded and showed him the poster. "This is the man I am looking for. Do you know him?"

The cowboy studied the picture for a moment. "Maybe so. I think he has been on the ranch before. Not right now but a while back. I'm the cow boss for the Upper Moon Ranch. He was hired to move some horses a few months back. After a couple of weeks, he disappeared with six of our best."

"Have you seen him since?"

"No, but I heard that he might be back in this country. My boss would sure like to see him again, you can bet on that."

"What else have you heard about him?"

"A sheepherder I know ran onto a lone rider a few days ago trailing three horses. Told him he was chasing strays for a ranch, sounds like the same guy."

"Do you have any idea where he might go if he didn't have horses in tow?"

"I remember him sayin' once that he had a place somewhere down by the Mescalero Reservation. I think he said something about a cabin the other side of Pajarita Mountain. It might be just bullshit though . . ."

Chapter 6

As Taylor rode into Mescalero, he tied up at the reservation's police office. He saw two men walking toward him, both were Apaches. Taylor recognized one of them as a man he had worked with before.

"José, it is good to see you again, you looking for outlaws?"

José nodded. "Hello Elan, it is good to see you too."

"This is my deputy, Taza, he has been with me for a while now. Taza, this is José Taylor, a sheriff from the other side of the Rio Grande." Both nodded slightly.

"I am looking for a horse thief," said José, showing the poster to him. "There is a rumor that he might be somewhere around the east side of Pajarita Mountain. Have you been up there recently?"

He shook his head. "Not for a while, very few people in that part of the reservation, it is very dry. Do you want to go for a look?"

"Yes. But I need food and a few supplies first."

"Come with me, we shall have a meal before we leave. Taza, will watch over things until we return. It should not be more than a few days."

Taylor always preferred to work alone, but the reservation required him to check in with the tribal police first. Elan would accompany him while on Mescalero property. In this case, he didn't mind. They had worked together before to capture an Apache murderer that had escaped from jail. Short and heavy, he was in poor shape to hunt down outlaws, but was a good tracker and knew the reservation well.

After a good meal of rabbit and turkey with fried bread and a drink made from the fruit of the mescal cactus, he handed him an extra canteen. "We will need to refill all the water canteens every chance we get."

He checked his horse and gear and tied on the extra water. "I am ready when you are."

Elan settled into the saddle and spurred his horse. "Good, then let us go find your outlaw."

After two hours of riding in the heat and dust of the trail, they turned up a deep wash and came to a cluster of cottonwoods. "We can get a little relief from the sun up here and there is water for the horses."

As the horses drank they rested in the shade watching a large, fast moving dust devil, race across the flat ground below them and disappear over a rise to the east. "That is a sign, José, it is showing us the way."

"Is that the way we are heading anyway?"

"It is, but we now know for sure, the dust is a good sign." Elan led them through the rocks and around the trees. Coming over a rise they flushed several deer heading down a well-worn game trail. Following the trail, they crossed a wide barren mesa and dropped down the other side into a thick forest. After an hour, they rode into a grassy meadow just large enough for the horses and the men. In the center was another spring, much stronger than most in the area and the remains of a lean-to cabin that would keep them out of the wind. "We will sleep here. The water is sweet and we are well sheltered. We can have a small fire tonight."

Running a picket line across the narrow end of the clearing, he tied on the horses and unsaddled them. He combed and brushed them while Elan started a fire. "Our meal will be ready soon. It is meat from the buck my son shot a few days ago."

"Thank him for the meat please; it is more than I usually have on the trail."

"José, I heard that you took a Navajo wife, is that true?"

"Yes. Her name is Sara Song, from the Ramah Navajo Reservation. Two white men took her from her hogan. I found her with them in a cabin in the Zuni Mountains."

"Was she okay?"

"She was fine."

"Did you bring the men back alive?"

"I brought them back, but they were not alive."

"So you kept this Navajo woman for yourself?"

"We were married by the medicine man. She is now on my ranch."

"Everyone knows those Navajo women are all crazy . . . If I knew you were looking for a wife, I could have got you a fine Apache woman for very little, maybe just a sheep or two."

"Thank you. I think one wife will be enough."

"You can bring an Apache woman back if you do not like her."

"Thank you Elan. I will remember that if I need a new one."

*

They moved out early the next morning. As they rode along an old deer trail on the side of a steep hill, the skies darkened and lightening began to crash all around them. Within minutes they were beaten down by ice cold rain. Spurring hard they rode full speed into the thickest stand of trees they could find.

Pulling on their slickers, they covered up as the storm got worse. With the horses tied to a tree, the men sat on the ground next to each other covering their heads. The rain pounded them hard and they held tight in their makeshift shelter for nearly an hour.

"José, that was a good rain, another sign that we are looking in the right place."

"You think that was a good sign also?"

"Yes, a very good sign. We need rain and it is a sign that we are on the right trail."

The rain and wind stopped as quickly as it started and blue skies showed between the trees. Walking the horses into a clearing, they decided to camp early and dry out the horses and the gear. Tying off the horses, José removed the saddles and bridles and spread the blankets and slickers over a clump of low bushes.

Elan started a fire, added kindling and fashioned a spit out of damp branches. Pulling out some deer meat from his bag he threaded it on the spit. He set a cloth bag full of roasted piñon nuts next to the fire and another bag with cactus fruit. He gathered some dead mesquite branches and broke them up for firewood. "We will be warm and eat well tonight my friend," said Elan, popping a few nuts in his mouth.

José looked at the meal he had prepared. "It looks very good. We can rest well on a full belly. We will catch up to our quarry soon."

"I think very soon," said Elan, as he pulled his hat down over his eyes. "Wake me when the meat is ready."

José sat down next to the fire and warmed himself. He watched as the horses soaked up the warmth, the steam rising off their backs as the sun did its job. After the meal, he threw the last of the wood in the fire and lay back on his blanket. The last thing he remembered was the faint fragrance of the burning mesquite.

Picking up the trail again, they moved slowly through the fresh mud. "That is Pagarita Mountain," said Elan, pointing at a peak to the north. "I would be surprised if he had much of a place to hide up there. The dry days have driven everyone to better ground."

"We should circle it and look for fresh tracks, this mud will help us."

Elan nodded. "We will start around the west side and see what we can find." Spurring his horse, he moved through the cedars and piñons pushing through the brush, keeping the mountain on his right.

For several hours the two men rode quietly along the flanks of the mountain looking for the tracks of a rider. They crossed the trail of deer, elk and small animals but no sign of a horse. "José, it is getting late, I know of a good spot just ahead to stop for tonight."

"We should keep moving. I want to catch up with him as soon as possible if he is here," said José. "If he was working alone he would have already been around the mountain, but he was bound to follow Elan's lead. He had to admit he liked having a little company but they were moving far too slowly for him.

After a quick breakfast of jerky and nuts, they were back on the trail. As they began circling around the north side of the mountain, they crossed a set of tracks from two shod horses. They headed southeast down the mountain.

"These are from yesterday. It could be your outlaw leading one extra horse."

Examining the tracks closely, he nodded. "It could be him; he may have stolen another horse on his way here."

"Maybe we can catch up yet today," said Elan, spurring his horse up the trail.

José followed at a distance scanning the hills and arroyos running down the foothills. Periodically he took out his binoculars and slowly looked over the country ahead of him. Game trails crisscrossed the hillsides winding in and out of the trees making it difficult to tell from a distance if any were made by horses. Elan had disappeared over the hill while he was scanning ahead.

Now is the time he needs to go slowly, thought José.

At the top of the hill he could see him in the wash, down on one knee with the reins of his horse in one hand. "He made camp here last night. He had two horses tied on this tree. The ashes are still warm. He does not know we are following him."

After surveying the scene for a minute José agreed. "We must follow him quietly and be sure that he does not detect us before we are ready."

"He has left a good trail, we should catch up soon," said Elan. Mounting his horse, he started off on the trail. As the hills flattened out, the country changed to rimrock and dry desert. The tracks were clear but the open country made it difficult to stay concealed. Like usual, in his excitement Elan had ridden far ahead of him looking for the outlaw.

José went slower, using what the country offered for concealment. After an hour on the trail he saw a rider coming toward him trailing dust. It was Elan.

He slid to a stop along side of him. "I saw him, he's just two ridges over. He is not moving fast; I think the horse he is leading was holding him back."

"Did he see you?"

"I do not think he saw me."

"We will see . . ."

Riding to the crest of the next hill, they watched the trail ahead until they were satisfied he was not close. They walked their horses ahead slowly and stopped behind a cluster of broken rimrock and dismounted. Crawling up to the rocks they looked down into the next draw. After a few minutes of looking over the area, they saw a single horse dragging a lead rope running through the wash. "He let that one go, he is on the run," said Elan, "I will go for our horses."

Standing up, he turned toward the horses and instantly fell over dead, his face gushing blood from a rifle shot to the side of his head. José heard the shot the same moment he fell. He saw a small puff of smoke drifting through some bushes across the draw. Crawling toward Elan he tried to pull him behind the rock. As he dug his heels into the dirt to pull, he felt a burning thud on his left heel and his leg popped up and twisted him around. Another bullet hit the dirt just below him.

From behind the rock he saw two more swirls of smoke and saw the dirt fly just below his feet. When the shooting stopped, he looked down at his boot. His spur strap was bent and the boot heel was mangled. His foot felt like it was on fire. Pulling off the boot was so painful he almost screamed out loud. The spur saved his foot from taking the full impact of the bullet, but his heel was bleeding badly. Wrapping his bandanna tightly around his foot he forced his foot into the bloody boot.

Three more rounds hit the sand and the rocks around him and then the shooting stopped for good. He saw a small cloud of dust behind the rocks. *He is leaving the country or he is coming around for me*, thought José. Finding a place to hide in the rocks, he burrowed down as far as he could and waited quietly until dark. When the rider didn't show himself, he crawled out and tried to stand. Pain streaked up his leg. He used Elan's rifle as a cane and put his own over his shoulder. Limping badly, he made it back to the horses. The foot was so swollen it felt like it would burst through his boot. He knew he could never load Elan's body on the horse in his condition. Untying the reins of Elan's horse, he pulled off the saddle and bridle and turned it lose to let it find its own way.

Holding onto the cantle and the horn, he pushed up with his right leg and mounted his horse. Riding around the end of the rocks he could see the tracks in the moonlight leading into the open country in the east. He knew he couldn't follow him and he couldn't leave his friend's body back in the rocks. His foot was still bleeding and the pain was getting worse as he rode back to the body.

Finding two long saplings, he fashioned a crude travois with four smaller crosspieces. He managed to get the body rolled onto it and put the saddle, bridle and Elan's goods on top and lashed everything down. Tying the poles to the sides of his saddle he climbed up and started heading north, to Fort Stanton. It was about the same distance as the reservation, but he could skirt around most of the rougher hills and mountains and stay on the flatter ground for easier travel.

For three days the sky had been clear and the sun unmerciful. He found water once and had finished the last of it that morning. In the afternoon of the third day he saw a large dust cloud coming his way. He'd been on foot leading his horse for the last day and they were both failing fast. Standing with his rifle, he waited to see what the dust cloud would bring. The first thing he recognized was the American flag and a detachment of troopers from the fort.

The captain of the patrol rode up to him and handed him his canteen. He nodded and took a long drink, "Captain, how far is it to Fort Stanton?"

"About five miles." Motioning for his troopers, they took his horse and helped him walk to the supply wagon. After lifting him in, they made him as comfortable as possible and laid Elan's body beside him.

He woke up in a bed wondering where he was. A tall heavyset man with long black sideburns and mustache looked down at him. "Deputy, good to see you awake. We've been a little worried about you, that foot is pretty messed up."

Looking down, he could see his toes sticking out of a thick white bandage. "Will my foot be okay?"

"I think it'll be good, but you will have a limp for a while. I think maybe the tight boot probably kept you from bleeding to death. I'm Alexander Dawson, the doctor for Fort Stanton. I had to cut away a thin piece of tissue on the outside of the heel where your spur strap cut into it and sew it back up. It should heal fine if you care for it properly. But the nasty bruise and the pain will be with you for quite a while."

"It does not feel as painful as it did."

"That's because I gave you an injection of morphine shortly before you woke up. When you are ready to leave, I'll give you some pills to take with you."

"What happened to my horse? And what of the body of my friend?"

"They've all been taken care of. The wrangler has been caring for your mount and a telegram has been sent to your sheriff to let him know you're here. Your friend has been given a Christian burial in our cemetery."

"I would like to speak to the fort commander."

"I'll let him know that you are awake. For now, just rest."

Chapter 7

"Deputy, I'm Colonel Elias Woods, commander of Fort Stanton, tell me what happened."

"I am Socorro County Deputy Sheriff José Taylor out of Magdalena. Myself and Elan Dasoles, the Mescalero Reservation Chief of Police, were on the trail of a horse thief named Pierce Miller. I was told to deliver him to you. They say he is a deserter, now he is also a killer."

"The patrol that you ran into was also looking for him. They had business east of here and were looking for that no-good goddammed deserter while they were out there. He stole four horses as well as money from the quartermasters safe. You say he killed your partner?"

"Yes. We were ambushed. He was concealed in some rocks and shot Elan in the head. He hit me in the heel. I think he left the country after that, but I could not follow."

A short man with a wild fringe of white hair sticking out from under his hat, Woods got red in the face as he talked. Now wheezing and breathing hard, he punched his finger in the air for emphasis. "That no good son of a bitch will not get away with this! If I have to send the whole goddamn western army after him I will! Trust me, that bastard will pay for this . . ."

After another day on his back, he couldn't stay put any longer. The doctor gave him a crutch and he left the hospital room in search of new boots. He found boots at the post store, but his left foot was too swollen to get it on. He bought a pair of tall black army issue trooper boots and two pairs of thick gray socks. Slitting the seam on the outside of the left heel to make more room, he pulled the sock on over the bandage and forced his foot all the way into the new boot.

For a moment he thought he might pass out. The pain ran back up his leg and made him wince. After catching his breath, he stood up and walked around the room several times. Leaning the crutch against the wall, he walked out the door.

Finding the corral, he motioned to the wrangler. "Someone brought in my horse two days ago. They said you were caring for him?"

"The big bay with the white socks?"

José nodded. "That is the one, will he be okay?"

"He'll be okay, but he needs a couple more days of rest and good feed." Walking the horse to the fence, he handed him the lead rope.

José looked in his mouth and checked his feet. "I think he is still sore in the back, but he looks okay after such an ordeal. Take good care of him and I will pick him up in two or three days, thank you."

His next stop was the telegraph office. The first wire was to his brother Andres, Station Master in Magdalena.

Brother, please send someone to the ranch and inform them I am okay and that it may be another week or two before I return. — José.

His second wire was to the Mescalero Indian Reservation police department.

This wire is to inform you that Chief Elan Dasoles was killed in the line of duty while attempting to apprehend a fugitive. He has been buried at the Fort Stanton army post.
—Socorro County Deputy Sheriff, José Taylor.

He stayed around the fort two more days, bought a few supplies and cleaned his guns. The doctor cleaned the wound and replaced the bandage each day. "Deputy, you should really stay at least another week so I can keep an eye on that wound."

"I have already lost too much time. The man who killed my friend is free and I have to bring him in."

"You will need to have the sutures removed in about a week."

He stood and reached his hand out to the doctor. "I will do it. Thank you for your help."

As he walked to the corral he was met by Colonel Woods. "You can't be serious, you're leaving already? That foot isn't even healed yet . . ."

"Someone has to find him — that is my job."

"It's too late deputy. He was caught trying to steal a horse over near Roswell, I just got the wire. I am sending a patrol to get him in the morning."

He thought about this new development for a minute. "Colonel, the murder took place on the reservation. I will need to take him to the Apache authorities, I am the witness."

"Deputy, I would have to argue that point. He deserted the army before these other crimes occurred, that would give us jurisdiction over him."

"I understand what you are saying, but Elan had a large family and was well thought of by everyone on the reservation, he must go back for a trial."

Woods nodded. "Okay deputy, I know the feelings involved, I really do. Here's what I can do. I will allow you to take him back, but I have to send a small patrol, just four men, to represent the army's place in this business. I will send the paperwork with you that will make everything legal."

"That will be okay. When can we leave?"

"The day after they return from Roswell. Will you need anything else before you leave?"

"I lost my binoculars somewhere along the trail. Do you know where I can purchase another pair?"

"No, I don't know where you can purchase them, but please take mine, the army has extras."

"I will need to pay you for them Colonel."

"Nonsense. You have done a great service for the army and this fort. These are a gift to thank you for your help from the United States Army."

*

José and the four troopers left the post with the prisoner shackled in a small wagon. The ride to the reservation was long and hot. Fine grit covered the men and horses and they stopped at a waterhole the second night on the trail. As everyone washed up and prepared for a late meal, the prisoner spoke for the first time. "So deputy, what did you think of my shootin' back there? That Injun' dropped like he was hit by a bolt of lightnin'; you were damn lucky I didn't get you too."

José picked up his rifle and walked over to him. "Stop talking — now . . ."

"What the hell, but he was nothing more than a filthy, murderin' Apache . . ."

Before he could finish talking, José drove the butt of his Winchester into his face with a sickening thud and the prisoner fell flat on his back, blowing blood in the air.

As the troopers finished their meal, the unconscious prisoner began to wake up. "What the hell did you do that for? I was just talkin'."

José squatted down next to him. "You killed my friend. I told you to stop talking about it."

"Goddamn you, I think you broke my jaw."

"Stop talking — now."

"Go to hell . . ."

For the second time the butt of the rifle connected with the prisoner's jaw and he went down again.

Two troopers sitting on the bed of the wagon saw him hit the man with his rifle. "If that jaw weren't broken before, it surely is now," said one of the troopers. "I don't think I want that guy looking for me."

"You're right about that," said the second trooper. "He's a mean little son of a bitch for sure."

Pulling into Mescalero he was met by Taza, the police deputy. After locking the prisoner in the one cell in the jailhouse, they carried Elan's personal property into the office. "See to it that his family gets these things, they are all Elan's."

"I will take care of it. Tell me what happened."

After repeating the story, he showed him the legal documents giving the Mescalero Reservation jurisdiction over the prisoner. "He is an army deserter and a thief. When you are through with him, he will need to be sent back to the army at Fort Stanton. When you put him on trial, I will come back as a witness."

"Trial . . .? Elan was a very important person to the Apaches," said Taza.

José shrugged. "Either way. If I can help with anything, wire me in Magdalena."

*

The next morning, he mounted up and headed for the ranch. His first stop was the Lincoln House in Ruidoso, to get a room. "You're back again," said the same Mexican woman he met the first time. "I hope your business went well?"

"My business was okay. I would like a room for the night. And I will be down for one of those steaks."

"Remember to be early, we have only twenty steaks today."

"Is there a place in town where I can bathe?"

"A block east and a block north, Miss Belle's Laundry."

"And a doctor?"

"Right across the street."

"I will be back for the key in a while."

Walking across the street he stepped into the medical office and waited inside the front door. A very thin man with a narrow fringe of red hair and wearing gold spectacles addressed him. "Can I help you?"

"Yes. The doctor at Fort Stanton told me I should see you when I came through. I was shot in the heel."

The man stuck out his hand. "I'm Doctor Timothy O'Byrne, have a seat and let's take a look." The doctor helped him get the boot off and pulled down the sock. Removing the bandage, he looked at the sutures and the bruise. Then he bent down, put his nose to the foot and smelled the wound. "I don't smell anything gangrenous, that's a good sign. The army doctor did a good job of sewing."

"Then my foot will be okay?"

"It's okay right now, but I would suggest allowing it to air out for a while, that is leave the boot and sock off. I'll clean the wound and give you a new dressing."

"I need to get a bath; will that be okay?"

"Two things. If you are going to Miss Belle's, make sure they give you clean water, sometimes they say it's clean but no telling how many cowboys have been there before you. Second, wash off the foot carefully but don't soak it too long. Those sutures need two or three more days before you take them out."

Pulling his sock and boot back on, he reached into his shirt pocket. "Thank you. How much do I owe you?"

"Dollar and a quarter. If I were you, I'd find a pair of moccasins to wear for a few days. Like I said, let it air out a while."

Limping slightly, he found the laundry and walked in. An older Asian man was behind the counter. "Is Miss Belle here? I would like to have a bath. And I would like a fresh tub of hot water. Can I get it here?"

The man nodded. "Yessir, you can, but there is no Miss Belle, just me and my daughter. It will take us a while to heat the water."

"That will be okay. I can wait. What happened to Miss Belle?"

"She returned to China; she did not like it here."

"I am sorry. Can you brush my clothes too?"

The man nodded. "Yessir, we can clean anything you need."

The water was plenty hot and he settled slowly into the large wooden tub. Rinsing off his injured foot he hung it awkwardly over the side. He didn't realize how sore and bruised he was and the hot water felt good. After he washed off and the water cooled, his clothes were waiting for him. He'd nearly forgotten how good the hot water felt the first time he tried it in Magdalena. Taking one of the morphine pills, he put the dressing back in place, pulled on his clean pair of socks, finished dressing and headed for the hotel.

"Cutting it close again," said the waitress. "You're steak number eighteen, I'll get your beer."

José rode out of Ruidoso just as the sun was rising. His first stop was the Mexican farmer. He had to deal with the three horses the outlaw left with him. Riding up to the corral he could see that the horses looked much better. Franklin and his wife had taken good care of them.

The farmer saw him tying his horse to the rail. "Hola, Señor Taylor, you caught the thief?"

"Yes, he is in jail. The horses look much better now."

"Si, they are ready for the road. Are you taking them today?"

"No. If it is agreeable with you, I will leave them here and notify the owners of their location. If they want them back, they will come for them within sixty days. If not, they are yours to do with as you please. Would you like to keep the horses?"

"Si, they would be a great help to us."

"I have written out a document you need to keep safe. If anyone questions why you have them, tell them to wire the Sheriff in Magdalena. Do you need more feed money?"

"No, you were more than generous the first time."

He shook his hand and mounted up. "Thank you for your help." He recorded the brand on the horses and rode out.

His next stop was the sheepherder. Riding up to the camp, he saw the man and two dogs working the flock toward the pen. The man waved and opened the gate, the dogs guarding against any escaping sheep. "Hola, señor, did you find the killer of my ram?"

"Yes, he is in jail. How much was the ram worth?"

"He was a good ram; he bred many ewes. I think a ram like that would bring four dollars."

José handed him the money, thanked him for his help and rode off.

After picking his way through the lava field again, he turned toward Socorro and several long days of riding. When he reached the Rio Grande, he stripped his horse and led him into the river to cool off and get fresh water. Sitting in the cool water, he lay back and submerged himself, washing away some of the misery of the ride. Making his way to the Socorro Railway station, he sent a telegram to Andres.

Brother: will be on the next train from Socorro. José.

*

Leading his horse off the platform, Andres took the reins from him.

"Brother, why are you limping?"

"I was shot in the foot, but it is healing."

"Did you get the man you were chasing?"

José nodded, "He is in jail."

"Good. Come to the house and rest a while. You can take a fresh horse when you leave, this one is clearly exhausted."

"Yes, he has done more work on this trip than any horse should ever have to do. Be sure he has fresh oats and he needs to have his feet looked at."

69

"Not to worry, we will take good care of him. You just come inside and rest."

"I think I could use a meal . . ."

"Marisol will take care of that."

Andres helped him remove his boot and sock. "This looks very ugly brother. I will have the doctor come and look at it while the meal is prepared."

"No need, the doctor said it will be fine. I removed the sutures three days ago."

"Lay down for a while. I'll let you know when supper is ready."

He woke up with Andres holding his leg and the local doctor cutting his boot off. "What is happening?"

"The doctor is checking your foot, lay still."

"I just bought those boots . . ."

Checking the condition of his heel, the doctor cleaned it and put on a fresh dressing. "You're lucky this didn't get infected. You have a huge blister right next to the wound. I cleaned it up and put some salve on it. You must leave your boots off for a couple of days then get a new pair that fit correctly."

"Andres, how long did I sleep?"

"Several hours. Marisol will make some food when you are ready. Father took your horse to the livery."

"I will rest a while and have a meal, but I must get back to the ranch tomorrow."

"Have some food and rest tonight. We will see how it goes in the morning."

"I need to check on my horses and the ranch. I will leave tomorrow."

Andres knew he would never convince him. Like always, his mind was already made up. "Okay José, whatever you say. Leave in the morning then."

After the meal, he lay down on a pallet in front of the fireplace. Marisol put a quilt on him and he fell immediately to sleep.

Waking up to the smell of fresh coffee, he felt better than he had in a long while. His foot still hurt, but not as bad as it did the day before. He took one of the pills the doctor gave him and limped to the table. Marisol kissed him on the cheek. "Good morning José, are you feeling well today?"

"Yes, thank you. I do feel somewhat better. Your wonderful cooking will help me even more."

"I have fresh eggs, ham, chilies and tortillas this morning, and the coffee is also fresh from the store."

José's father, Heck, now gray-haired and retired from the railroad, sat down across from him. "You will pay your respects to your mother before you leave?"

"You know I will father. How have you been?"

"I'm just a worn-out old Mexican railroad man. I am glad to have a soft place to sit and a pretty señora to make my meals."

"Andres says that you still cut firewood and enjoy reading. I think you are not as worn-out as you say."

Marisol put her hands on the old man's shoulder and kissed him on his forehead. "He is not as worn out as he says, he can be a bit grouchy though."

At noon, Andres came in for an afternoon meal and sat at the table with them. "You are still here? I thought you would head out with the sun."

"It is your wife's fault. She made me eat too much. Then father started telling stories about mother and how they came to be here. It was good to hear the old stories. And now it is time to eat again, and here I am."

"After the meal I can look for new boots. Father, will you come with me?"

Heck nodded. "There is a fine Mexican boot maker nearby. He has many in his shop, we can find some there."

"That will be okay. We will pass by the cemetery; I can pay my respects to mother." Cutting the damaged boot down to a few inches high, he put on a clean sock, he pushed his foot into it and wrapped it with a rag to hold it on.

He hated to go to the cemetery, even after all the years that had passed. They stood over the stone marker that read:

Shan Shan Taylor
Beloved wife of Heck
Mother of José and Andres

It always made him sad to think about the murder of his mother, and it was one of the few times he ever showed any emotion. "She was such a special person," said Heck, his tears starting to flow.

José nodded and slipped his arm around the old man's shoulder.

"I miss her so much. I think I will see her soon."

"Not too soon father, we still need you here."

They walked into the store and Heck introduced him to the boot maker. "This is my son, José. He needs new boots, but the left one may need special work because he has an injury."

The boot maker, a middle-aged Mexican man, asked to see the injured foot. "It looks like it is still swollen señor. Perhaps you should wait a while before you buy?"

"No, I have to be on the road tomorrow. What can you do to help me for now?"

Looking over the boots on the shelf, he chose a tall, black pair and handed them to him. "Try on the right one."

He pulled it on. "This is a good fit. What about the left one? It will be too tight."

Going back to the shelf, he picked another pair identical to the first one but a larger size. "Try on the left one."

The left boot went on easily and felt good. "This is okay. How much?"

"You will have to buy both pair señor. When the foot is healed, you will have two good pair of boots."

"I do not need two pair if one will not fit properly."

"If you take both pair now, and want to return one pair after the foot is healed, I will give you three dollars back. I can sell them as used boots."

"He will take them," said Heck. "José, when the time comes bring them to the house, they should fit Andres."

Walking back to the house, he limped slightly, but the large boot and thick sock felt good. "Father, I am leaving in the morning, but I will come to visit more often."

"We are always happy for your visits."

Chapter 8

José stopped at the sheriff's office before he headed to the ranch. After he told the story of the murder of Elan and the arrest of the killer, he gave him a drawing of the brand on the three horses he left behind and directions how to find them. "It looked like a C with a cross over it."

"I know this brand," said Davis. "It's the mark of the Center Cross Ranch up north of here. I'll send them a wire telling them where the horses are so they can recover them if they want to."

"Be sure and inform them they must pay the sheep farmer for his trouble. I will be on the ranch for a few days. Is there anything that you need me to do?"

"No. Go home and rest. I'll let you know if something comes up."

Passing under the sign that read *Taylor Horses,* he rode into the barn. Stripping his horse, he turned him into the back pasture.

"Hello boss. Good to see you back, is this a new one?"

"Hello Albert. No, this one belongs to Andres. Mine was worn out and he is taking care of it."

"Did you find your outlaw?"

"Yes, he is in jail. How are the horses doing?"

"They are all good, things have been quiet. Did you get hurt? You appear to be limping."

José nodded. "Shot in the foot, but it is healing. How is my new wife?"

"She is wonderful. Everyone is in love with her. She is already like a long-time member of the family, and she is proving to be good with horses."

Sara Song saw him through the window and ran out to meet him. Throwing her arms around him she began kissing him. "My husband, I have missed you. We all thought you might be hurt when you did not come home right away. Come inside and have some food and tell us about your trip."

As they walked into the house she noticed him favoring his left leg. "What did you do to your foot?"

"I was shot in the heel . . ."

"You are shot? Sit down in front of the fireplace and I will look at your foot."

"I am okay, it is nothing."

"Sit down. That is why you have a wife, to take care of you."

He sat down on their bed and put his legs on a stool while she pulled off his boots. "The doctor said it will heal okay."

Removing the dressing, she washed his foot. Then she mixed up a damp, smelly clump of grassy looking material and put it on the blister, wrapping it with a rag. "This is what the Navajo Medicine Man uses to heal such things. You leave it on while the fire warms you."

He pulled her onto the bed next to him and kissed her. "Thank you, my beautiful wife. No one has ever taken care of me like this before."

"Like I told you once before, your eyes must be clouded to think that I am beautiful." Pushing away, she moved his legs onto the bed and put a quilt over him. "Now you sleep. When you wake up we will get you cleaned up, you stink."

"I will just clean up in the creek."

"Go to sleep, we will talk about it later."

When he woke up it was dark, and the cabin smelled like chilies and frijoles. "Wife, where are you?"

She walked into the bedroom with a lantern in her hand. "I am here. How are you feeling?"

"Much better than the last few days. Supper smells good, is it ready?"

"It will be ready in a few minutes, but it is now the morning meal. You have been asleep a long time, the sun will be up soon."

Pulling the quilt off, he unwrapped the rag around his heel. The blister did look much better, the new skin felt much softer. When he stepped on it for the first time, the pain was still there, but not as bad as before.

"Husband, does it feel better?"

He nodded. "It is less painful this morning."

Helping him get his sock on, she walked with him to the table. Laura set a cup of steaming coffee in front of him. "Mr. José, how are you this morning? Did you catch your outlaw?"

"Yes, he is in jail."

"And you got shot in the foot?"

"In the heel, yes."

"And you are leaving again soon?"

"No, I want to spend a few days with the horses before I go."

Sara Song smacked him playfully on top of his head. "With the horses? You would prefer to spend your time with horses over the woman you say is so beautiful?"

"Well, I guess I could spend part of the time with you . . ."

She hit him again. "Those horses will not feed you or keep you warm in your bed at night, you would do good to remember that."

"I promise I will remember that," he said, cracking a rare smile.

"Now eat your meal. I have a surprise for you when you are finished. She led him to a large wooden tub behind the house near the creek bank. "Albert said you bathed in a tub in town. I saw this old horse trough in the barn and asked him if we could make a bathing tub for us."

"You want me to bathe in a horse trough full of ice cold water?"

"No. I want us to bathe in a proper way, like they do in town. Albert found a large metal tub and set it by the creek above us. The water flows into it, a fire underneath it heats the water then it flows through a pipe down into the trough. I asked him to build a fire when you woke up."

"Am I that dirty?"

"When was the last time you bathed?"

"I wash up in the creek every day."

"There is more to proper bathing than just hands and face. You are filthy and you stink. Now strip and get in. Laura will bring you clean clothes."

Stepping up to the tub full of water, he lowered his good foot in to test it. "It is hardly warm, not hot at all."

"Husband, get all the way in and I will show you how to make it hot."

When he settled down into the tub she released a piece of rope holding a section of pipe up against a cottonwood branch and lowered it to the trough. A stream of hot water rushed in. Pulling the pipe back up, she took off her dress and stepped in. "Is it hot enough now?"

"Yes, it is good. Are all Indian women as clean as you?"

"All Navajo women like to be clean; we are not like those filthy Apaches." Producing a large yellow block of soap and a rag, she motioned for him to turn around so she could wash his back. After she gave him a good scrubbing, she handed the soap and rag to him.

"Now it is your turn to clean me." José pulled her closer and kissed her on the lips. She pushed back gently. "Clean first, then fun."

Washing her body was another new experience for him, one that he liked. "Wife, you are right. You are much better company than a horse . . ."

Between spending time with her, the hot baths and working with his horses, he enjoyed the week at the ranch more than ever before. It was the first time in his life he was ever hesitant to leave home. When he went to town for supplies he stopped at the sheriff's office. "José, how's the foot today? You think you're ready to go back to work?"

"It hurts a little, but I am ready."

Davis handed him a poster. "This is one in particular that I need you on. He robbed a bank in El Paso and another one a week later in Las Cruces. He shot up that one pretty bad and shot two bankers, somehow they both lived. In El Paso, he managed to kill a couple of horses and wound one citizen when he rode out."

"I will bring him back. Has anyone seen him since the Las Cruces robbery?"

"No, but the sheriff down there says he has family in the area, including two brothers with a violent past and a father just like them."

"Did they try to find him?"

"They said they did, but had no luck. I don't think they wanted to take on the whole clan. Truth is, I don't think they wanted to find him at all, I think they want you to find him. They know your reputation and that you can find the bad ones."

"That is okay with me. I will find him and bring him back."

"Take him to Las Cruces when you get him. They'll work out some kind of a deal with the El Paso guys. And keep your eyes open for Texas Rangers, they may be looking for him too."

"This is New Mexico Territory; they need to stay down there."

"They'll try and take him back to Texas if they find him first."

"They will not find him first . . ."

He shoved the paperwork across the desk. "Here's the warrant. Send a wire when you get him."

The poster had a decent likeness of him and a good description. The warrant read:

WANTED:

Cletus Case Daniels – AKA - Case Daniels
In: El Paso, Texas. Bank robbery - attempted murder
In: Las Cruces, New Mexico Territory. Bank robbery
– attempted murder – two counts
36 years old – 5'- 10" – 175 lbs. Right-handed

Known to be armed and extremely dangerous
Known to carry two pistols
Last seen in the Las Cruces area
Apprehend - dead or alive deliver to Las Cruces Sheriff's office

"I will leave tomorrow. I have to go back to the ranch tonight."

"José, there's one other thing . . . I just heard the Indian is in the territory . . ."

"Where was he last seen?"

"Word is that he was spotted near Santa Fe and he was chased south by several ranchers and they lost him. You want the paperwork now?"

"Yes. The sooner I find him the better for everyone."

Pulling a file full of papers out of his desk drawer, he handed it to him. *Indian Jake LaSalle* was written on the side. "There's a lot of information about old crimes and places he's been. There's an old poster picture that's not too good and several warrants in there too. José, I know I don't have to tell you how dangerous this man is . . . he's been operating alone for nearly fifteen years. The man has murdered lawmen, women and children and escaped from captivity several times. None of the tribes up here claim him as one of theirs, but some think he's a Texas Comanche. The rangers say he's a mixed-blood Comanche, but no one seems to be sure. He's been stabbed at least once and shot a couple of times. When they caught up to him the last time he had the scalp of a blonde woman on his saddle," said Davis.

"I will find him," said José, reading over the paperwork.

"José, the days of all that Wild West crap that people back east like to read about are all but gone. This country is settling in. He really is one of the last of the bad ones."

Jose' put the paperwork in his pocket. "Let me know if you hear anything else. I will go after him after I find Case."

*

José lay back on the bed with Sara Song in his arms. He turned off the lamp and let the soft flicker of the fireplace light the dark room. "Husband, will you always be leaving me like this?"

He pulled her closer. "It is what I do. I track down outlaws and bring them in for trial. I do not really know what else I would do."

Slipping off her dress, she laid across him, pulling the blanket over them. "You are an expert with horses and you know all about cattle and ranching."

"I could do that, but I like this job and I am still young enough to do it. Perhaps in a few years I will be ready for a change, but not yet."

"But what if something bad happened to you? What would become of your family?"

"There is only you, and a woman so beautiful would not find it difficult to get another man."

"What if there was more than just me?"

"Why would there be more than just you?"

"Husband, for a man so smart you do not pay much attention to me."

"Why do you say that?"

"I laid across your chest, did you not notice my body?"

"I am in bed with a beautiful woman, how could I not notice your body?"

"Give me your hand."

He stuck out his hand and she placed it firmly on her stomach. "Can you see that my belly is getting large?"

"Well yes, I thought it was because you were eating more."

She sat up in the bed and stared at him. "Husband — you are very frustrating. I will give you one more chance to give me the right answer. Then you will have to find some other Indian woman to warm your bed, maybe you can buy some nasty old Apache grandmother."

Slowly it came to him what she was saying. "You — you are going to have a baby?"

"Yes, we are going to have a baby, you will have more family now." They lay back on the bed and made love in the warmth of the fire.

"I love you Sara Song. I never imagined I could find someone like you to be my wife." They lay together for a long while, kissing and caressing each other. "I understand why you are concerned about me," said José. "I will start thinking more about our future. We will need room for our children and our animals. I think we should consider a ranch in Colorado for our home."

"Why in Colorado? What is wrong with this place?"

"If I give up the Deputy Sheriff job, I would like to have a larger ranch and raise horses, cattle and children. There are many beautiful places in the mountains up there, a lot of good grass and plenty of water. It is also much cooler for my animals."

"And when do you plan on finding this new ranch way up in the mountains?"

"I already have one. I was in Colorado several years ago and found a place I liked, so I bought it."

"And you didn't think to tell your wife about it?"

"I had it before I knew you. I did not think it important enough to bother you. After our son is born, we will take a trip there for you to see it. We can now take the train all the way to a Colorado town called Fairplay, my land is close. I have to leave for a trip tomorrow, it will take several days. When I return, we can talk about Colorado."

He kissed her one more time. "Always be on the watch while I am gone. Sometimes we get questionable looking people wanting work or a handout. Isaac has become very good with his rifle and Albert knows to watch for strangers around here. He has a shotgun in the house and one in the barn. You also have the pistol if you need it. It uses the same cartridges as Isaac's rifle."

"As long as we can be together as a family, Colorado will be okay with me, I love you José Taylor."

He tied the last of his gear on his saddle. He hugged her for a long time and kissed her goodbye. "Husband, you had better come back to me and do not get shot again . . ."

"I promise I will come home uninjured. I need to be with you when our son is born."

"You have decided it will be a son?"

"It will be a son. We will have a daughter right after."

"You sound very sure about that."

He mounted up and turned to leave. "I will be back soon."

Chapter 9

After he left, Sara Song sat in front of the fireplace with Laura and Albert. They shared a pot of tea while the fire began to crackle. "Tea was something José learned to love when he was a small boy," said Laura. "Did you know his mother was Chinese?"

She shook her head. "I know little of his life before he rescued me. I thought he was a Mexican from south of the river."

"His mother came to America from China with her family and settled in El Paso. She married a man from somewhere in southern Mexico. You already know his father, Heck, he was the railway station master here in Magdalena and was for many years and is now retired. His other son, Andres, runs the station now. They both got their love of tea from their mother."

"He has said little about his mother and father to me. What was her name?"

"His mother's name was Shan Shan. Also a beautiful woman with two names like you. She is buried in the town cemetery."

"That is a beautiful name."

Laura poured them more tea. "They say she was one of the most beautiful women in the territory. Heck was also very handsome. They say that is why their two sons are such handsome men. The story goes that both of their last names were long and confusing, so before they had their first child they decided to choose a new name, one that sounded American. They chose Taylor from a sign they saw on a livery in town."

"Then some monster murdered her," said Albert. "Raped and killed her right in her home. José was very young and working way up in the mountains as a cowboy then, but he went after the killer. A week later he caught up with him in a remote little town called Alma, down in the southwest part of the territory. The man's name was Garo Tompkins, a well-known outlaw. When José saw him walk into a saloon, he followed him in with his rifle. The witnesses say one minute later they heard a single shot and the outlaw was dead. Nobody knows for sure what was said in the saloon, but they loaded him up on his horse and José hauled him all the way back to Magdalena."

"It is sad to lose your mother like that, I lost my family too," said Sara Song.

"It was very sad," said Laura. "He was a very bitter and angry man for a long time after. He took the job as a deputy for the county when they couldn't find anyone else to do it. For several years after that, he was always alone. All he did was hunt down outlaws and take care of his horses."

"Now he has become very famous as a man-hunter," said Albert. "Everyone knows that if he is after you, it is better just to turn yourself in. More than one outlaw has done that."

Sara Song nodded. "I have seen that some people are afraid of him when they find out who he is, and I have seen him at work."

Laura poured the last of the tea in her cup. "This is Lapsing, our favorite, please have the rest of it. He also gained a reputation for being very cold and very dangerous within his duties as a deputy. Outside of his job, he is still a quiet loner, but he has softened a bit since he bought this place and began buying and caring for his horses."

"It is good he could buy this ranch and have a place of his own."

"Yes," said Laura. "He puts all his pay right into the bank. He rarely spends anything except for his horses. Now and then he checks with the bank to make sure that everything is good. He has been doing that since he took the job."

"How did you and Albert come to work for him?"

"When he bought this ranch we worked for the old owners. We didn't know what we would do when he bought it. When he took it over, he asked us if we would stay and work for him. It was a blessing for us. The day after he moved his horses out here he had to go on a trip, he just trusted us from the start."

"He is a very good man," said Sara Song.

"Yes he is. But we were very surprised when he brought home a wife. For a long time, he could hardly even speak to a woman."

"He usually is quiet," said Sara Song. "Sometimes he seems very trusting. He was slow to catch on that I wanted to be with him. I did everything I could to get him to take notice of me."

Albert and Laura both laughed out loud at the idea of a woman convincing José Taylor to take her for a wife. "Sweetheart, you are the best thing that has ever happened to him. We thought he would never find a woman and be alone forever. He is a hard man to understand. He needed something soft and gentle in his life, someone to care for him, and you are perfect."

"He has you and Albert, I know that is a great help."

"He is very good to us, and we all care about each other, but it is not the same as a wife and children. We are now complete. We all have a family now and we are excited about one day having children in the house."

Chapter 10

José tied up his horse in front of the Las Cruces Sheriff's Office. Walking into the office he sat down at the sheriff's desk. "Good to see you again José, you want some coffee?"

"No. I came to see you about Case Daniels. What can you tell me about him that is not in the warrant?"

Sheriff Travis Tucker poured himself a cup of coffee and started to roll a fresh cigarette. "Well, he's a natural born piece of trash. He's been in one kind of trouble or another since he was a kid. He's also dumber than a pile of horseshit. In El Paso, he walked into the bank without even a bandanna to cover him and stuck a pistol in the teller's face. He ran out with just twenty-one dollars to find his horse gone, he forgot to tie it to the rail, so he stole another horse and shot a citizen on horseback when he got in the way."

"Then he came back to Las Cruces to rob this bank?"

Tucker nodded. "I guess he needed more money, because a week later he shot the hell out of the First Territorial Bank and wounded two tellers, all for less than forty dollars."

"Any thoughts as to where he might be hiding out?"

"The Daniels family is well known in the ranching business. They have a lot of ground spread all over the east side of the

Manzano mountains. I knew the father pretty well a long time ago. His name is Kennedy Daniels, a big intimidating looking guy with a long droopy mustache. He's kind of a shady character to say the least. Rumor is that he created his herd out of stolen calves and cows and got most of his land through crooked dealing."

"None of them have been arrested before?"

"All of the boys have been arrested more than once, but never convicted of anything. Most of the arrests were for theft and brand violations, and some for fighting and killing sheep. They are so isolated and spread out that they can hide stolen stock all over that part of the territory and no one can find them. I can't imagine why Case robbed the banks, he must've been drunk and got a wild hair up his ass. They have plenty of money for lawyers. I figure the family is hiding him out in one of those places."

"Thank you. I will bring him back."

"José, this guy may be dumb, but he's dangerous. He has two brothers, Alan and Bob. They're just as dumb and just as dangerous. All three are kind of a nervous, twitchy bunch, you need to keep an eye out for them."

"I will be okay."

"I can give you a deputy to ride with you if you want."

He shook his head. "I work alone, a partner is just someone to take care of."

Following the Rio Grande north for a day he swung east skirting around the south end of the Manzano foothills. The flat, dusty country had been home to many generations of Indians, most of them long before his time. Riding through the ancient ruins and broken foothills he turned toward the mountains. Settling in for the night he built a small fire and cooked a rabbit. He also boiled a cup of water for tea, a rare luxury for him. Tomorrow he would start the hunt for Case Daniels.

After several hours of riding slowly into the rising sun, he stopped to scan the countryside with his new binoculars. Spotting smoke from a small campfire, he cautiously approached until he could see a family of Indians gathered at a small water hole. He rode up to the camp and held his hands up for the family to see. They looked like Apaches tending to a small flock of sheep.

Within minutes he was invited to sit and share a meal with them. When they finished, he thanked them and pulled out the poster and asked if they had ever seen the man in the picture. With a mix of Apache, English and Spanish, they explained to him that, no, they had not seen him, but if he were to look farther up north there was a ranch with several white men that were known to treat Indians and Mexicans badly. "They kill our sheep and chase us from our land," said the oldest man in the group. "You might find him up there. If you go in to Manzano, there is a store that provides supplies to ranchers and to Indians. They would know about the white man."

José thanked them for their help, mounted up and headed north. That night he moved into the tree covered hills and set his camp without a fire. Eating jerky and nuts, he took a swallow of water and lay his head on his saddle. He was up just before daylight and sat on a side hill letting the sun warm him while he scanned the countryside finding nothing.

The next morning, he repeated his search moving farther north and west. In a short time, he found a small herd of cows filtering through the cedars and piñons. Two riders watched from horseback as the herd fed slowly down the hill. Both were Mexicans and didn't match any of the information on the Daniels men.

He gave the men a wide berth and continued north, making a note to himself where the water was if he needed to come back. Manzano was a small collection of run-down adobe huts, corrals, one well, with a new windmill for stock, and one squat, rough adobe building with a log and sod roof. It had a crude sign that identified it as a livery, cantina and dry goods store.

Tying his horse up at the trough, he watched the building for several minutes. Indians and Mexicans appeared to be the only people using the store, most likely the only people in the whole place. Pulling his rifle from the saddle, he headed for the store. Inside he waited a moment for his eyes to adjust. It was dark with a low ceiling and smelled of wood smoke and cigars like most of these places. Several oil lamps lit the room and a small fire burned in the fireplace.

"Hola, señor, how can I help you?"

"I need something to eat and some information," said José.

"Come sit over here in the corner. I can get you some fresh tamales, or some frijoles and tortillas if you prefer . . ."

"I would like some tamales."

"We have only whisky and water to drink."

"Water."

When the man brought out the food, José set his rifle on the table, motioned for him to sit and showed him the poster. "I am Deputy Sheriff José Taylor. I am looking for a bank robber, he is a white man named Case Daniels. I have been told he might be around here. They say his family has a ranch around here somewhere."

"Si, the Daniels family live up in the hills. There are several sons and this could be one of them."

"Have you seen any of them recently?"

"No, but the mother and father were here about a week ago. I think they were on their way to Albuquerque. They had a wagon and two of their men on horseback with them. They bought a few supplies and left the same day."

Finishing the tamales and the water, he dropped two dollars on the table. "How do you get to the ranch?"

"Straight west perhaps ten miles. After you get into the trees and hills be very careful, the sons are not good people. If they see you coming and see that you are the law and a Mexican, they can be very violent." Pushing the coins back the man shook his head.

"Señor, it is less than a dollar for the food . . ."

He nodded. "It is okay, thank you for your help."

riding slowly, he headed west on the trail through the flat country. As he approached the first of the hills he turned south for a mile then continued west. Slowly, he moved from tree to tree looking for signs of people or cattle. As the terrain got steeper he would glass from the next ridge then move to another. After a day of searching, he found a spot under a high rimrock overhang where he could spend the night out of the wind.

Continuing the search before sunup, he spent several more hours tediously picking his way toward the main ranch. The hills were covered with scrub oak and mesquite bushes that were thick and full of long sharp thorns. Cowboys called them devil trees and they made travel slow.

As he approached a particularly steep hill, he heard the faint sound of cattle bawling. He tied up and crawled to the crest, looking down the other side. A long, narrow valley was filled with cows and one white cowboy on horseback watched from the far side. A small spring-fed pond, surrounded by thick grass and cattails, filled one end while a narrow ribbon of a stream ran down the valley. Three more horses were picketed above the pond and a teepee was set back in the trees. Leaving his horse, he hiked around the end of the valley and stopped directly above the tent.

Watching the man on horseback through the binoculars, he looked similar in age and appearance to the one in the picture, he needed to see him up close. Concealing himself in the rocks above the tent, he settled in and waited for him to come in for the next meal. As the sun began to set, a lantern suddenly lit up the tent and another cowboy crawled out. He threw some wood on the remaining coals of the fire and soon had something cooking.

While the food cooked, he saddled a horse and got ready for his shift. Spotting the fire, the cowboy on horseback made his way back to the tent. Stripping the saddle, he tied up his horse and sat down by the fire. He decided the man that rode in was Case Daniels and he was glad to find him so quickly, this country could keep him looking for days. The other man was likely to be one of his brothers. Finishing their meal, the second cowboy headed out to take his shift on night watch and Daniels crawled into the tent.

After waiting for complete darkness and for the fire to die down, he heard the man begin to snore. Moving quietly to the back of the tent he listened for several more minutes, then slit the back of the canvas tent open and stepped in.

Watching him snore for a minute, he looked at him closely and confirmed it was his man. Pressing the muzzle of his rifle directly under his chin he pulled back the hammer. The click woke Daniels up. "What the hell is this?"

"Be very quiet," said José, pushing the muzzle tighter into his throat. "I am Deputy Sheriff José Taylor. I have a warrant for your arrest for bank robbery in El Paso Texas and Socorro."

Daniels stared up at José, shocked that someone had found him. "Screw you . . . You ain't taking me anywhere, my brothers will kill you first. All I have to do is yell for my brother and he'll come running. He'll kill you right away."

He held the rifle steady against his throat. "Here is what will happen. You will not make a sound while you saddle a horse. Then we will get my horse and I will take you back to Socorro."

"And if I don't?"

"I will put a bullet through your heart. When your brother hears the shot, he will come to see what it is about, and I will put a bullet through his heart too."

"He didn't have anything to do with the robberies . . ."

"I do not care."

Pushing him through the hole in the tent they walked to the horses. After the prisoner saddled up they made their way up the hill leading the horse. When they reached José's horse, his prisoner mounted up and José shackled him and tied his hands to the horn. "This is very simple; you try to escape I will kill you. Then I will take you back tied over the saddle."

He led them up the next ridge behind the tent and dropped down into the valley. The moon was covered by fast moving storm clouds and they rode quickly for the next hour. As the rain started and the wind picked up, he began to look for shelter. Remembering the ruins he saw on the way in, he headed for them.

Reaching the remains of several stone buildings, he rode through the doorway of a burned-out church and tied up the horses. Huddling in the corner of the tallest remaining walls and under a low stack of fallen timbers, the two men waited out the storm. The church wall kept them dry but the horses were taking a beating. Chewing on a strip of elk jerky, he kept his Winchester across his knees pointed at his prisoner.

As he reached into his saddlebag for more jerky, a bullet hit the back wall and chunks of broken stone rained down on both men. Another shot splintered one of the timbers. Both men dug down into the timbers for better cover. José peered out between the timbers at the horizon. Daniels suddenly crawled out and jumped up and started screaming, "Yeah —over here! Bob, It's me — I'm here . . !"

José jerked him back down into cover. "That's Bob, that's my brother . . ! I told you he was gonna kill you, you're a dead man now!"

José poked him in the chest with the muzzle of the rifle. "Sit there and shut up or I will kill you right now."

As they stayed down in the cover of the timbers, the rainstorm moved out and the sun began to heat up the landscape. He wrapped the prisoner's shackles around a solid timber and turned back to the horizon. The area was full of piles of scattered ruins and the shooter could be in any of them.

"Deputy, you let me go and Bob won't kill you. He just wants to get me outta here."

Before he could respond, two quick shots fractured more stones on the back wall sending more pieces of rock through the timbers. "Do what I told you or I will kill both of you."

When the sun lit up the church ruins, the heat became unbearable. Crawling to his horse he took his canteen off the saddle. It had just enough water in it for a day if they used it sparingly. Giving the prisoner the first swallow, he took a drink himself. "Not much left in there deputy. I know my brother will have plenty, it's time to give yourself up . . ."

97

As he watched the ruins in front of him, the prisoner started to scream. "He's done Bob! Kill him now — get me outta here!"

Two slugs instantly thumped against the pile of stones. This time José spotted a puff of smoke come out of a large pile of loose stones and rubble. He stared hard through his binoculars at every stone and scrap of wood in the shooters cover. Picking out cracks and small spaces in the pile of stones, he estimated the distance at just over a hundred yards. Shoving the barrel of the rifle out between two rocks he steadied for a shot.

The rifle jumped sideways through his hands before he could fire. The prisoner had kicked the side of the butt. He looked back at him lying there with a smirk on his face. "Can't let you shoot my brother . . ."

He jerked the rifle butt straight back and caught him in the throat. "I told you to be quiet, do you want to die?" Lining up the sights again he waited for a moment until he had his breath right and the sight was steady. He picked out a narrow opening between the stones where he saw the smoke and squeezed the trigger. He heard a muffled scream from the rocks. His bullet had found its way through the space in the rocks and glanced off one of them, finding its mark.

The shooter hollered from the rock pile. "Goddamn you lawman, I'm gonna kill you! Can you hear me you son of a bitch?"

Firing again at another opening in the rocks he heard another scream. He knew that both shots were not likely to be deadly wounds, but they might be enough to cause him to make a mistake. He decided to wait and see what he would do next.

His wait was short. The shots came fast and wild, hitting nearly everything but José and the prisoner. One bullet glanced off the horn of his saddle and another went through the tail of the outlaw's horse. He picked out another opening and fired.

"Not this time lawman, it's a clean miss . . ."

He fired twice more into openings in the rock pile then reloaded and watched. When the sun began to set, he waited to see if there was any sign of life from the shooter. When it was dark, he checked his rifle and looked at his prisoner. "Not one sound." The prisoner nodded.

After a long night, just before the sun came up, José crawled out of the fallen timbers, through the legs of the horses and out of the church ruins. He kept low and made a long loop around the shooters cover. Approaching a low rock wall, he could see the man's legs and lower body sticking out from the end of the stones. Crawling further along the wall, he saw him lying on his side with his left arm and leg straight out, his right arm under him and the other leg bent back nearly touching his hip.

He kept his rifle on him for several minutes, waiting to see if he moved. Tossing a rock at the man he waited. When he got no response, he walked the last few steps toward the body with the rifle trained on him. Before he could check him, the man rolled over, jerked out a pistol from under him and swung it wildly toward José.

Squeezing the trigger of his rifle at the same moment, the bullet drove through the center of Bob Daniels chest killing him instantly.

José fell on his back, feeling a burning sensation on his side. The pistol bullet had hit his rifle stock, glanced off and grazed his ribs slightly, ripping his shirt and drawing blood. Walking back to the ruins he stepped inside and took the reins of the horses, moving them outside.

"Deputy, what happened out there? Tell me what the hell happened, goddamn it!"

"Bob is dead."

"You son of a bitch, I have another brother and he'll find your sorry ass — you piece of crap. I guarantee he'll kill you for sure! You also gotta deal with my old man, he ain't gonna stop 'till you're dead, you hear me?"

"He can pick up your brothers body at the funeral home in Socorro. After they hang you for the bank robberies, he can pick up yours there too."

Gathering up all the horses he moved them to a small ditch with water that ran through the ruins. Under an ancient stand of cottonwoods, he stripped the gear off and tied them alongside the ditch. Making a small meal they ate quietly, the prisoner no longer talking. "You will help me load your brother's body on the horse and we will head back to town. Nothing has changed," said José. "You run and I'll kill you."

Remembering the wound on his side, he looked at it in the firelight. He decided it didn't look all that bad and wrapped his extra shirt around his chest. He would check with the doctor in town if it still bothered him. Remembering his promise to Sara Song that he would not get shot again, he wondered what she would have to say about this.

Preparing the body for the horse, they realized why he hadn't moved from the spot where he fell. One of José's first shots between the stones had glanced off and hit him in the kneecap, shattering the joint. It didn't bleed enough to kill him but he couldn't move far dragging one useless leg.

Reaching the Rio Grande, he stopped to water the horses before going into town. Walking into the sheriff's office, he led his prisoner into the cell, slammed it shut and removed his shackles. Sheriff Tucker walked over to the cell and looked at the prisoner. "Case, just what the hell were you thinkin'?" The prisoner shook his head and pointed at his throat.

"He is not talking good right now," said José. "He will be better when he goes to trial. His brother Bob is on the horse outside. All the gear is on their horses. You should get him to the undertaker soon."

"You killed Bob? How the hell did that happen?"

"They were watching a herd near a waterhole up in the Manzano foothills. I got Case while he was sleeping in their tent. We got away quietly and rode hard for an hour or so. I ducked into some old ruins to get out of a rainstorm. When Bob saw he was missing, he tracked us to the ruins and had us pinned down for a day."

"So you shot Bob from where you were pinned down?"

"Yes. As you said, they are not very smart."

"José, this could be real bad for you."

"Why do you think that?"

"Kennedy Daniels just had one son killed and one going on trial, and that one might get hung. How do you think he would feel?"

"That is his problem, I just did my job."

"It won't much matter to him that you were just doing your job . . . he's a dangerous son of a bitch, he's likely to come looking for you."

"If he comes, I will deal with it."

"Just make sure you and yours are safe . . ."

He nodded, dropped the paperwork on the desk and headed for the door. "Where is your doctor at?"

"End of the road, just around the corner to the left," said Tucker. "You hurt bad? I can see you're limping some."

José shook his head."

"This ain't hardly nothin'," said the doctor, applying a dressing to the wound on his ribcage. "However, it's gonna leave a scar."

"A scar is okay."

"What about that limp? Anything I can do for it?"

"It is an old injury to my heel; it has already healed."

"Take your boot off. You're already in the doctor's office, I just as well check it out."

"Okay I guess."

Sliding the oversized boot off, the doctor pulled the foot onto his lap. "It's healed, but it has a formed a small knot, or lump under the area that was sewed. Nothing I can do here, but if you ever get to a big city, you may find a surgeon that is able to fix it."

"I will live with the limp."

"How did you get the injury?"

"I was shot."

Chapter 11

"Husband, you said you would not get shot again," said Sara Song, looking at the wound on his ribs.

"It is just a small scratch. I want to have a meal and then sleep for a while and I will be okay."

"Laura is preparing the meal right now, then we will get you clean and put you in the bed."

"You mean in the horse trough?"

She nodded. "Yes husband, it is time." After bathing in the trough and having a long soak, they walked back to the ranch house with Sara Song holding onto his arm tightly.

"Do you plan to bathe me every time I come home?"

"Yes. Do you not want to be clean?"

"Being with you in a trough full of hot water is something I like. If I have to be cleaned while I am there, that is okay too."

Walking into the cabin he noticed several changes. Albert had built a mantel above the main fireplace and two jars full of wildflowers were sitting on it. Both fireplaces in the cabin had been built long ago and never had a mantel put in place. The kitchen had been whitewashed and fresh flowers were on the table. "This is different . . ."

Laura and Albert watched his face for his reaction. "Do you like it Mister José?" asked Laura.

Nodding, he looked at the flowers and whitewash. "Yes. This is okay, I like this."

Still holding onto his arm, she led him into their sleeping room. Albert had built a mantel for their room too, and more flowers covered it. Above it he had put two wooden pegs two feet apart and one longer peg on either side of the fireplace. His freshly brushed hat hung on one of the pegs and his Winchester rifle hung on the two pegs above the mantel. His pistol belt and spurs hung on the other side.

The small window in the end of the room had new glass in it and a red curtain covering it. "Albert found a new piece of glass. He said it had been broken for a while, and I made a curtain out of some old cloth."

"It is good, I like it, thank you wife." He pulled her close and gave her a kiss. Looking at the bed he asked her if something was different about it.

She kissed him back, holding it for a long moment. "Yes husband. We have cleaned it and washed all the bedding. They were all filthy, just like you when you come home from your trips. Now, when you return, you bathe before you get in bed and it will stay clean."

"We both just bathed, can we go to bed now?"

"After the meal husband. Then we can go to the room for the night."

*

José and Albert watched as Isaac ran six horses into the small pen. One at a time Isaac hooked a rope to the halter and led them to the fence tying them off. José looked over each horse from top to bottom, inspecting the feet and checking the teeth, making notes on the horses' general condition.

"Albert, I want to brand these tomorrow. You and Isaac get things ready in the morning, I have put their information in the book," said José. "There are three stallions, I want these two cut," pointing to two off to one side. I think the tall bay will make a good stud. The other three are mares. Also, I have changed our brand." He handed him two new irons, both with a new rafter SS design. "We will use these on all of our horses from now on."

The next morning the three men built a small mesquite fire near the corner of the pen. When it was burned down to a good bed of coals, Albert stuck the new irons in. Turning one mare into the pen José gathered up a loop and waited for his moment. When the mare swung around Isaac rushed in and grabbed the throatlatch with both hands and held tight. The horse spun him around the pen like a rag doll but he never gave up his hold. When the horse began to slow down, Albert threw a long loop and expertly gathered in the front feet and dallied off keeping tension on the rope. With Isaac and Albert pulling, they laid the colt down in the pen.

When the dust began to clear up, Isaac, still holding on to the halter, swung up on the mare's neck, twisting the young horse's head backward and held it for several minutes. Horse and man were engulfed in a thick cloud of dust and a test of their will power.

José caught the hind feet with another loop and pulled tight while Albert quickly jumped off his horse and tied the front feet and hind feet with a short piece of rope and the mare stopped fighting.

Pulling the iron from the fire, he took the few steps to the horse, now calmed down in the dirt, and planted the rafter SS iron on his left flank. A few seconds later he pulled it away in a billowing cloud of burning hair. Pulling the half hitches from the feet, everyone backed away. After several seconds the horse began to kick and roll. She stood up and kicked her hind end up in the air several times and made several laps around the pen. It was the first in the Sara Song line of horses. Albert brushed off his hat before he put it back on. "Isaac had a pretty good ride there, boss."

"Yes, but he is a little light for a big horse like that . . ."

"Shoot boss, that was fun," said Isaac. "Still five more to go!"

Sara Song watched at the fence as they finished up with the horses. "I came to see if you men are ready for a meal."

"We are, do you like our new brand?"

She looked closely at the nearest horse. "What does this mean?"

"It means Sara Song. We will use it on all our horses from now on."

"Husband, it is beautiful that you did that, but you know I cannot read your letters very well."

"I have thought about this," said José. "I think it is important to learn to read and write the language, so I asked Laura if she would start teaching you while I am away."

She hugged him tightly. "Thank you husband, that is two gifts I received today, I love you."

José kissed her on the cheek. "I think we are all hungry, then we will have a talk."

"What are we talking about?"

"Colorado."

After a good meal of fresh beef and potatoes from the cellar, she sat down next to him at the table. "Husband, do you want to move to Colorado right now?"

"I am very dirty from the horses," said José. "I think it would be better to discuss it while we were bathing . . ."

She thought about this for a moment, then her face lit up in a big smile. "Husband, I think you are making a joke to me, I like that. Okay, now it is time for talk. When do you want to move to the mountains of Colorado?"

"Maybe in one or two years. When our son is born, we can decide. There is one thing that I have to do as a deputy before we move."

"The outlaw Indian? You still want to go after him?"

"There is nobody else to do it."

"They say he is very dangerous, and he will kill anyone who comes near him. No one has been able to stop him for many years."

"That is true. But he never had me hunting for him."

"I think we should move soon and let someone else catch him."

"This is my job. It is something I have to do."

*

José sat down for the evening meal with the family. "I am preparing for another trip tomorrow. But first I have to talk to you about something. After my last trip, I delivered the outlaw to the Las Cruces sheriff. Before I left, he said I could be in danger from his other family members. If I am in danger, that means that you could be in danger."

"Everyone must be constantly alert for strangers around here.

Albert, do you have plenty of shells for your shotguns?"

"Yes boss. I have plenty, and I will pay close attention."

"Isaac, you have plenty of shells for your rifle?"

"Yessir, I am ready."

"Sara Song . . ."

"Yes husband, I can shoot the pistol. And I have my knife."

Chapter 12

Sheriff Davis sat back in his chair reading the local paper and smoking a cigar. "José, you sure this is something you want to do right now? I know your foot is still hurting."

"It is okay. When I brought the outlaw to the sheriff in Las Cruces he said to watch for his father and brother and maybe some of their hired men. They may be looking for revenge. Here is some information from Sheriff Tucker about them. He said to wire him if you see them or they cause any trouble."

"I'll keep an eye out. I'll check on things at the ranch too."

"Thank you. Do you have any new information on Jake?"

"A little. Last word was that he'd been spotted somewhere around the west end of the stock driveway. There are so many cattle, horses and sheep on there at any given time, that it's an easy place to steal a few. An old cowboy friend of mine was in town a few days ago. He's been riding for the slant bar 7 ranch west of Aragon. He said there's a rumor that he's been hanging around the area and grabbing a couple of cows or sheep and selling them to some of the local Indians. The stock guys won't go after him because they don't want to take a chance someone will get hurt and the Indians won't talk about it, they need the meat." He handed the paperwork to José. "I had everything updated. I don't think there's anything he's not wanted for."

"I will find him."

"José, I know we've talked about this before, but the Indian is different than most outlaws. He started on his rampage many years ago and I don't see anyone bringing him in alive. It might be best to keep your identity hidden. If he hears of a lawman in the area he will probably come looking for you. Most outlaws want to get away from you. Jake lives for the chance to kill you."

"I will find him, and I will bring him in."

Andres and Heck sat at the table with José and studied the warrant. "Brother, you do not have to be the one to do this. There are other deputies. We all worry when you leave for a trip."

"It is my job. Another deputy with less experience is likely to be killed. No, it has to be me."

WANTED:

Jake LaSalle: *AKA – Indian Jake LaSalle — Indian Jake*
Wanted for multiple murders in Texas and New Mexico Territory
– attempted murder, horse, cattle and
sheep theft – arson - assault
40-50 years old - 5' 8" tall – 150 pounds – long gray/black hair
– bullet scars on abdomen and upper right chest and
4" knife scar above right hip – missing right thumb
Heavily armed and extremely dangerous

Recover subject dead or alive
Deliver subject to nearest secure detention facility

*

José sat on his horse next to the railroad cattle pens. After talking with the cow boss, he arranged to ride with his crew to pick up a herd of cattle and drive them back. He would be a working cowboy for the ranch and when they started to return with the herd, he could watch for the Indian along the way. If he saw him, he would drop out of the drive to pursue him.

The Magdalena livestock driveway was an old trail a hundred and twenty-five-miles-long, several miles wide, and ran from Springerville Arizona, to the stock yards in Magdalena. Railroads had not reached any farther west and tens of thousands of cattle and sheep were trailed along the driveway to be shipped out at the railhead every year. John Casum, the cow boss for the Double A Ranch, and two of his hands waved at him. Catching up with the cowboys, they headed for Springerville to pick up the herd.

"Good to have you along. Ever do much of this cowboy work?" asked Casum.

"Yes. My brother Andres and I spent several years working at ranches around here. He now runs the Magdalena station."

"Andres? Your father is Heck Taylor?"

"Yes, he is my father."

"Well I can tell you this, your old man is one of the best men I ever met. He has done a thousand things for me and all the other cattlemen around here. How's he doing these days?"

"He is well. A little slower than he used to be, and a little deaf, but Andres and Marisol take good care of him."

"Good, I'm glad to hear that. Andres does a great job now. Tell him John Casum says hello."

"I will tell him, thank you."

After passing a few herds heading east, and a long uneventful ride to Arizona, the team picked up several more day workers, seven hundred steers and a few dozen dry cows and started back on the trail. The first day was long and slow, making five miles at best. At chuck, they sat around the fire and told stories while they finished their meal. Throwing more wood on the fire, several rolled smokes and leaned back against their saddles.

"Well, for goddamn sakes!" said Casum loudly, startling everyone. "I just realized — you're José Taylor! You're the famous man hunter! You always come back with your man."

"I am Deputy Sheriff José Taylor, but I do not think I am famous."

"Oh, you're famous all right, everyone knows you. You and that rifle of yours have cleaned out half the outlaws in the territory. It's great to ride with you! So, you're here chasin' old Injun Jake?"

"I am. He has been on the loose too long."

"You gonna shoot that old son of a bitch in the heart like you usually do?"

"If he is shot or not is his decision. If he gives up, I will take him in alive."

"Do you really think that nasty old son of a bitch is gonna give up without a fight?"

"No."

The next day's drive covered nearly ten miles. Things went smoothly all day. The cowboys kept the herd together and they stopped in a well-watered valley with plenty of grass. After chuck, two nightriders started their shift. José and Casum lingered at the fire a little longer to talk.

"José, you're not a paid hand here, you can skip night watch if you want."

"No, it is okay. I have done it many times before; I will take my turn."

"Whatever you want to do is fine, I'm turnin' in."

After his two hours on shift, he lay back on his saddle and slept until he smelled the coffee. The trail cook, a cranky old Irishman named Donal, boiled a big pot of water, threw in a double handful of coffee and let it boil a few more minutes. A tin cup full of his boiling hot coffee had a nice thick layer of grounds in the bottom. When Ben, the first trail hand with enough courage to speak up, asked him why there were so many grounds in the cup, the old man walked over and poured more boiling hot coffee in his cup, spilling plenty in his lap. "It'll put hair on your ass and lead in your pencil. Don't insult the cook — got it boy?"

Ben jumped up and danced around a minute trying to keep the coffee from burning him. "Hell Donal," said Casum, "I doubt he's got a pencil big enough to put any lead in. Can't speak to the hair on his ass though, never had the opportunity to check that out . . ."

The cowboys all burst out laughing and choking, spitting the boiling coffee all over themselves. That night Ben became the official source of humor for the rest of the trip. Laying back on his saddle, José realized that he missed this. Though always a very private man, he remembered how he liked to hear the talk around the campfire when they were on the trail. When he took the job as deputy, he became even more of a loner by necessity. Now he had a family, and a lot more to think about.

On the fifth morning of the drive, the men moved the herd into a narrower stretch about a thousand yards wide with piñon and cedar covered hills on either side. Deep washouts ran down the sides into the flat ground. Recent rains had turned the pass into deep mud making it slow and difficult to navigate. The cattle were bunching up at the front and those at the rear were starting to wander. The cowboys chased stray after stray through the trees and out of the mesquite bushes. When the sun dropped, there were still several missing.

Sitting around the fire, Casum asked how many head they thought they'd lost. "I think we're missing four head boss," said Ben.

Casum looked at José. "Think this could be our Indian ?"

José nodded. "This would be a good place for him to do it. I will see if I can find his trail in the morning."

"You can take Ben with you, he's a good tracker."

"No, I will do this alone. If they are just strays, I will get them back for you. If it is Jake, I do not want anyone getting hurt. Right now, he does not know that a deputy is on this drive, that will be an advantage."

"Okay, it's your call. Good luck."

José rode out well before daylight, moving up the side hills. Riding slowly, he looked for any sign of riders or cattle. He saw where the cowboys had chased the strays the day before and turned them back. By the time the sun was high, he found the trail of one unshod horse, and several cows heading north. Moving a few yards off to the side of the tracks he began to parallel them.

For several hours he followed the trail. At times, he would stop and get down to study the tracks more closely. He continued the same slow methodical routine with little more than a few swallows of water and a few bites of elk jerky.

Resting his horse at night when he could find water, he'd sleep an hour or two and was back on the trail. On the afternoon of the second day he reached a long rocky ridge. Tying up his horse, he crawled up to the top with his glasses. Scanning the next valley, he saw something red in the bottom of the wash.

Stopping short of the wash he glassed everything in the area before he exposed himself. Stepping from behind the last tree he walked up to a bloody scene. One of the steers had been butchered and the bloody head, legs, hide and gut pile were scattered all over the dirt. The sun had been burning down for hours and the coagulated blood and body parts were alive with flies and crawling insects. *Just this morning*, José said to himself. Two horses had been on the scene. One with shoes carried a heavy load west. The other, unshod with a small split in the left front hoof, went northeast with the remaining three cows.

Back on the trail of the unshod horse, he pushed on in the scorching afternoon sun. For another five miles he repeated the same routine, losing the tracks over rocky ground then picking them up again through the sand and cactus covered desert. For another full day, he pursued the Indian.

Early the next morning he could see what looked like another bloody patch of red across the next wash. Carefully circling around, he sat on his horse at the edge of the trees from a hundred yards away looking at the spot through his glasses.

His horse dropped straight to the ground under him, shot through the head before he even heard the report. When he realized what was happening, he rolled off the horse and grabbed for his rifle. It was pinned tight under the dead horse. He pulled his Colt and cocked it, scanning the hillsides for his adversary.

Another shot hit the horse in the chest, punching a hole in the fender of the saddle. Two more rounds hit the horse in quick succession. He lay tight against the back of the horse with the Colt in his hand waiting for the shooter to show himself. When the shooting stopped, he heard a series of shouts and screams coming from across the wash. Peering over the horses neck he saw a lone figure on foot about two-hundred yards away, screaming and dancing and cursing him.

Indian Jake LaSalle was dressed in fringed leggings and a filthy oversized white shirt with a black cloth around his waist and a blue cloth around his head. He screamed at José for several minutes. "You coward lawman — you son of a pig and a buzzard — what happened? Have I killed you? Are you dead yet? Did you think I could not kill you?" The Indian danced and sang and taunted his enemy. Holding his rifle above his head. "I have killed many men better than you; you are not as good as a drunken old Apache woman . . ."

He lay still, watching the performance and waiting to see what he would do next. The Indian disappeared for a moment then reappeared riding his horse. "Do you see me lawman?" Riding back and forth he kept shouting, waiting for an answer.

José lay perfectly still with his pistol cocked, never taking his eyes off him. As the Indian summoned up his courage, he rode closer and closer still shouting. "Are you dead lawman? I think you are dead already or why would you not shoot at me?"

He knew that without his rifle, he could never reach him that far away with only his pistol. He had no choice but to wait and see if he would come near enough. As he got closer he estimated the yardage as still slightly out of range. The Indian stopped just short of pistol range and continued to taunt him.

Placing the barrel of the Colt across the saddle he waited until the Indian stopped moving. Raising the sights of his pistol two feet above his head to make up for the distance, he squeezed the trigger. The slug caught the Indian in the hand holding the rifle smashing two finger's and splintering the stock. The Indian screamed and cursed, dropping the rifle and spurring his horse at the same time. "You are going to die you son of a swine. I will find you and I will kill you and all of your family — you are all dead!" Then he was gone.

Releasing the cinch, he began to pull the saddle from under the dead horse. Sitting down and placing his feet on either side he pushed on the horse and pulled on the saddle at the same time, dragging it out. Checking his Winchester, it was dirty but looked no worse for the wear. His canteen was under the horse and smashed beyond repair. Taking the saddle and the rest of the tack he hung it in a piñon tree so it would be protected and he could find it later.

Still on the watch for Jake, he picked up his bags, slicker and rifle and started to walk. When he got to the bloody site where the steer lay, he could see it had been killed for no other purpose than to draw attention. Blood was spread all over the ground around it. He walked over and picked up the Indian's rifle, the stock was damaged and bloody but the rifle was still functional. He put it in the tree with the other gear.

Staring at the tracks of the horse the Indian rode out on, there were blood drops on the trail. Then he realized that the horse the Indian was riding was shod. All this time he was following the one without shoes. It finally came to him, the Indian switched horses at the last place where he got rid of two steers. His partner took the unshod horse and two steers, those were the tracks he had been following. There were no prints of the riders on the ground, they had changed horses without getting off. He had been fooled by the simple switch. The second Indian took the other steers and the unshod horse. Jake had set up watching the trail and José had ridden right into it. Indian Jake was proving to be a much better adversary than he had anticipated.

Walking south, he had covered several miles when he spotted the tops of several cottonwood trees behind a low rise. Cautiously, he walked up the rise and looked over. A dozen dead and dying trees were clustered around a pool of murky brown water ringed with green algae. Moving toward the water, he flushed out a doe and a fawn that were gone before he could get his rifle to his shoulder.

Stripping off his boots and socks he sat down and put his feet in the water, even as dirty as it was, it felt good on his bad foot. Pulling a little jerky from his bags he chewed it mindlessly, wondering how long it would take to walk out of this place. He estimated at least twenty-five miles to any known water. Starting a fire, he pulled a small tin cup from his bag and dipped it into the water. When the fire was down to coals, he set the cup in it and waited for it to boil. It would be his first water since his confrontation with the Indian.

Chapter 13

Sara Song asked Albert if it was usual for José to be gone so long.

"Sometimes, Missy. I think he will be along soon, don't worry."

"I will give him one day then I will go to find him . . ." Picking up firewood for the stove, she saw a single rider coming toward the cabin. It was Andres. Throwing his reins across the rail he walked toward her. "Andres, why have you come all the way out here? Did something happen to José?"

"I don't know, but a cattleman named Casum told me this morning that he was with him until about ten days ago. When they got to a place called Cattail Bottom, they lost four steers and José took off on their trail. They think he might have spotted the Indian."

"We will go now and find him . . ."

Andres shook his head. "No, it is too late today. We will leave at first light. You stay here, Albert and I will go."

"No, I will be ready to go when you are."

"This will be a long hot dirty ride; it would be better if you stayed here with Laura and watched the ranch."

"I will be ready to go with you in the morning. We will bring an extra horse and extra water; he may need them."

Andres knew it was no use to argue with her. He also knew she was good with horses and experienced in traveling the desert country. "Okay, you will come too. Meet us at the stock pens at sunup and we will leave then."

The three riders rode west passing two herds of cattle coming from Arizona. When they reached the spot called Cattail Bottom, they found a large flock of sheep filling the valley. Riding over to the Mexican pastores, Andres spoke with them in Spanish for several minutes. He knew most of the herders from working with them at the station. He had helped all of them over the years. When he was done, he told Sara Song and Albert that they had been invited to share a meal and camp there tonight. "The sun is almost gone. We will eat and sleep good tonight, and start out in the morning."

"We must leave early in the morning." said Sara Song. "My husband is in trouble and he needs me."

"We will leave early, Missy," said Albert. "José is the strongest man I have ever known; we will find him."

After a good meal of roast mutton, frijoles and tortillas, they fell asleep around the campfire with the pastores. Like every morning, Sara Song was the first to awaken, long before it was light she had the horses and gear ready to go. "Andres, Albert, we must get ready," she said, shaking them awake with her foot.

A cup of camp coffee and a piece of jerky was their breakfast. Andres thanked his hosts and they rode north looking for sign. Fanning out across the north hillsides, they rode back and forth gradually working their way to the top. Albert shouted at the other two, waving them over to him. "Here on the backside of the hill are tracks of two horses, one shod and one unshod. Also, a few cows were with them. The one with shoes is over top of the one without and those of the cows."

Andres climbed down and looked closely at the tracks. "It is good that we did not have any rain for two weeks or these would be gone. They are only here because they are protected from the wind. The exposed tracks have already dried up and blown away."

Looking around, Sara Song was gone, already on the trail. When they caught up with her she was down on one knee looking at something in her hand. "What do you see?" asked Andres.

"Elk jerky. It is like Albert makes at home. José must have dropped this small piece while he was tracking his outlaw."

"It is what I made at home," said Albert, tasting it.

Sara Song was already riding ahead, looking for the next piece of the trail. Finding another spot with signs of a campsite, she saw several hoof prints disappearing down the valley. "He was here, maybe the first night. The tracks are going northeast."

"You cannot be sure that he was here," said Andres. "There are a lot of people that could have left this."

She shook her head. "He was here."

"Are you sure, Missy?" asked Albert.

"He was here. Go whichever way you choose; I'm going this way. If he is injured or on foot, he will try and follow his own tracks back to the place where he knows for certain there is water. The closest place is where we camped last night."

Andres couldn't disagree with her logic, but the idea of this Indian woman leading them on the search bothered him more than a little. He would follow her lead for now, but if he didn't agree with her he would go his own way.

Following the pieces of broken trail, they rode up to a low rocky ridge and stopped to scan the valley for the next tracks. There were several ravens circling a dark spot in the bottom. Without saying anything, Sara Song headed into the valley. Sliding to a stop in the bottom, she jumped off and bent over the remains of a butchered cow.

Stopping next to her, Andres and Albert looked at the pile of bones and hide. "Looks like the first steer to go," said Andres.

"Someone cut this one up and hauled it away." She squatted down and pointed to the ground. "Look, right here. There are parts of three different hoof prints. One with shoes and one without go north. One with shoes goes west, more heavily loaded."

For the rest of the day they followed the scattered sign of the north trail until at the last light of the day they came on three sets of tracks in the bottom of a wash. José's tracks ran out at the edge of the wash, leaving the other two mixed up in the middle. They rode a wide circle trying to find any sign of the trail.

Andres rode back into the wash announcing that he had found hoof prints about half a mile out. "I found the trail, it is to the west, we need to go now . . ."

She paid little attention to him, laying the side of her head on the ground and looking out from the ground level. "The trail is this way. The ground is packed deeper here and goes to the northeast, I will go this way."

Andres shook his head in frustration. "It is this way. If you do not want to come that is okay. Albert, are you coming with me?"

"I am going with her." Turning his horse, he spurred hard and disappeared over the hill. For the next several hours they followed the rapidly disappearing trail as it led them farther to the north. In one spot, there was a print of an unshod horse with a clear horseshoe print on top of it. "We are close to him," said Sara Song.

They rode slowly back and forth covering every possible place that a man could be concealed. Looking close at every rock and bush, she was convinced that José was close. Pulling out her Colt, she fired it three times and listened for any sound. She reloaded, repeated the signal again and waited.

Now on foot leading her horse, she walked between the cedars and around large clumps of mesquite bushes looking for any sign. On the backside of a cluster of broken rock, she spotted a yucca plant that was trampled, and part of a boot print next to it. Then she heard it, three faint shots in rapid succession.

She reloaded and fired three more times as they began to walk slowly through the trees and washes. The terrain and the wind made it difficult to determine exactly what direction the shots came from. She fired three more rounds and waited. Three more shots rang out, much closer now. They moved faster, trying to pinpoint the sound. This time she didn't have to shoot, they heard three more rounds, this time very close.

Riding into the next wash, they could see a cluster of dead wood and branches that had been pushed up against the bank from some previous flood. Sticking outside the branches was a tall black boot. She jumped from her horse and started pulling off the branches. "Husband, are you there? Talk to me . . ."

"I am here wife, you have found me," said José in a low, scratchy voice. When they finished pulling away all the deadwood they could see his rifle barrel sticking out with his hand still gripping it. His face was badly sunburned and his eyes nearly swollen shut. His lips were grotesquely dried and cracked. Albert began to pour water on his face, gently rubbing his lips, trying to get him to open them enough to take water in.

Removing his heavy jacket and vest, they laid him out flat and gently pulled off his boots. "I lost my hat somewhere; do you have my hat? That is why I got sunburned. I need my hat."

"It is okay husband; we will find you a hat." Looking at his left foot, it was badly swollen and bright red. She poured some water on it and rubbed gently. He winced the moment she touched it. She rubbed the cream of an aloe plant gently on the heel and on his face.

"I do not think I will do much walking for a while. I kept stumbling and falling. I will get better now that you have found me."

"Missy, he won't be able to ride the extra horse," said Albert. "I will make a travois for him."

As she tended José, Andres rode in. "You found him!"

"Albert and I found him; you should have listened to me."

Andres nodded. "You are a good tracker. I did not know."

She changed the subject. "We will stay here tonight and see that he gets plenty of water and as much food as he can eat. He will sleep comfortable in the travois covered with blankets. Andres, you need to make a fire. I will make a shade to keep the sun off him."

That night she slept next to him, waking often to check on his condition. By morning some of the swelling in his face had started to go down. He was able to talk better and tell them what had happened with the Indian and his attempt to walk out. "After he shot my horse I was not able to get to my rifle. I had to wait for him to get close enough to shoot at him with my pistol. When I fired, I hit him in the hand and he ran away bleeding. It was a very lucky shot."

"I stripped all the gear from my dead horse, put it in a tree and started to walk. My canteen was destroyed so I had no water and the only place I knew to find good water for sure was where I left the cattle herd," he said, shifting uncomfortably in his bed. "I walked perhaps a full day and found a little water at some cottonwoods, but it was bad. I boiled water one small cup at a time until I was replenished and slept in the shade of the trees that day."

"Were you able to get food?" asked Albert.

126

He shook his head. "I had a little jerky and one apple in my bags. I could not catch anything else. I did not want to shoot for the first couple days. I did not want any Indians to know where I was.

I started walking again but my bad foot was too swollen and I needed water. After a few days, I was walking on the edge of the arroyo and fell off the edge. I stopped walking where you found me."

Sara Song wiped his face with a wet rag and stroked his hand.

"How many days were you walking when you sat in the branches?"

"Three or four, I am not sure. The branches in the arroyo may have saved me. Twice it rained somewhere up high and water came down the gully cooling me off and providing me a little water."

"Did you kill the Indian ?" asked Andres.

"No. That shot would not have killed him. I failed to bring him in, I will have to go out again."

"Husband, you will be going nowhere for a long time. You have to get healthy first."

"I will get healthy, but I will get him too."

*

Reaching Cattail Bottom, they stopped to camp for the night. José was beginning to feel better but he couldn't put any weight on his bad foot, or even touch it, it was still too swollen and painful. The nearest doctor was a hundred miles if they went back to

Magdalena, or about twenty-five if they went to Springerville. "We will take him to Springerville, it is closer. Albert and I will take him there. Andres, you can return to town. Please explain to Laura and the sheriff what is happening."

"Yes boss," said Andres.

For two days they rode slowly, tending to their patient. As he gained his strength back he told Albert that he wanted to ride.

"Missy, what do you think about putting José in the saddle?"

"No."

"Sorry boss," said Albert, with a grin.

Late the second day they rode into Round Valley and the dusty cow town of Springerville. Stopping at the sheriff's office, Sara Song told him about José, the Indian and needing a doctor.

"I know José Taylor by reputation only, but he is one of us and we will take good care of him. Come with me."

At the doctor's office, they helped José onto the table.

"José, it is an honor to meet you," said the sheriff, holding his hand out. Everyone knows what a famous lawman you are."

"Thank you, but I do not consider myself famous."

"That's okay, we all do. This is Doctor Peters. He'll fix you up."

The doctor listened to the story as he examined him. "Mister Taylor, you're in pretty good shape considering what you've been through. The foot however is a problem. Leave it like it is and it will never get any better than it is right now. And the more you use it the worse it will likely get."

"Will he be able to walk?" asked Sara Song.

"Yes, but it will be painful and he will need, at the very least, a cane, or maybe crutches."

"There is no way to fix it?"

"He has a large, hard lump under the scar. It's caused by some kind of growth from the old injury. It has to be removed, and I would suggest doing it as soon as possible."

José sat up and took her hand. "Can you do this thing doctor?"

"Yes, we can do it first thing in the morning. However, it is not something that I would typically do by myself, but you're in luck Deputy Taylor. I have a friend in town that is just passing through and he is an excellent surgeon. The two of us will take good care of you."

She grabbed him and held him, beginning to cry softly. "I was afraid, I thought you had been killed."

"I am safe, you have no need to cry."

She nodded and put her head on his shoulder. "Husband, you promised to kiss me and tell me you love me every day, I am ready now . . ."

He leaned over and kissed her and told her that she was beautiful and that he loved her.

"Thank you husband, I love you too."

"Doctor, I am ready for you to fix my foot," said José, sitting up on the table.

"José, this is my friend and colleague, Doctor William Packard, fresh from his recent training in new surgical techniques in New York. He came here just to show me the latest advances in the surgical world. Together we will fix your foot. Just lay back and we will put you to sleep."

"But I am not tired doctor."

"Just lay back, I will take care of that part." Placing a leather inhaler cup over his nose and mouth, the doctor shoved in a wad of gauze and poured in a few drops of chloroform. Within minutes he was asleep. "Would someone care to assist me? I will need you to administer the chloroform slowly until we're through."

Sara Song stepped in and took the job. Within minutes, the doctors had made a large incision across the old wound. They peeled back the skin to expose the lump. "Doctor Packard, have you seen anything like this in your experience?"

"No, I haven't. It is some type of calcified growth growing on the cuboid bone at the site of the injury and pressing on the calcaneus bone next to it.

"Doctor, what do those words mean," asked Sara Song.

"Basically it's like a bone that grew very fast due to an injury. We will have to try and saw the largest piece off and then file it down smooth, do you agree Doctor Peters?"

"I do. Do you think it will come back?"

"That's hard to say, but we can give him immediate relief for now."

After more than an hour of surgery, José woke up with a mild headache but little pain in his foot. "Will my foot be better now doctor?"

"It should be much better, and you will be able to get around okay. You will need to use a crutch when the pain goes down, at least for a while."

"It does not hurt much right now."

"That's because I gave you a big shot of morphine before you woke up. You know about morphine?"

José nodded. "I have had it before when I was first shot."

"You were shot?" said Doctor Packard.

"That is what happened to my foot. An outlaw shot me."

"Well, I have to say, that is a first for me."

"Welcome to the Wild West, Packard," said Peters.

"After three days in Springerville, José could not stand the noisy little town any longer. Each day the doctor checked his foot and changed the dressing. "You need at least three more days before you can travel Mister Taylor. You can't bounce around in a saddle for days. You can't take a chance that the stitches will pull out."

"He will not be in the saddle doctor," said Sara Song.

José shook his head. "I have to return home, there is work to be done."

"He will not be in the saddle doctor," she repeated.

"Well, whatever you decide to do, be sure he comes in tomorrow for a clean dressing."

When they returned to the hotel, José tried to explain to her that he was all right to travel.

"Husband, if you insist on this then I will make it so. But you must stay here, and Albert and I will be back later."

José nodded and lay back on the bed. "There is no way for me to go anywhere while you are gone."

"That will be good."

The next morning they helped him down the stairs and out the front door. Tied to the rail was a well-used buckboard with two horses hitched to it. In the back was a bed of straw and a pile of blankets. José looked over the outfit. "Where is the other horse?"

"We traded him for the buckboard," said Albert. "These two were the best match."

"You cannot ride in a saddle," said Sara Song. "So you will ride in the back and not hurt your foot. We will stop at the doctor and have him look at it before we leave.

The first two days were dusty and bumpy but uneventful. When they set camp in the bottoms, it was late afternoon and they just got the fire started when it began to blow and rain. The three climbed in the back of the wagon and covered up with a canvas tarp. After a few minutes the storm blew through and the sun came out hotter than before.

Albert climbed out of the wagon and pointed to the sky. "Look boss . . ."

A spectacular double rainbow graced the sky and they all watched it for a few minutes. José sat on the tailgate with his arms around Sara Song.

"A very good sign is what my friend Elan would say."

"He is right, it is a very good sign."

"Wife, you are with child!"

Turning to face him she smiled. "You had forgotten?"

"As I said, when I am working I can only think of the job. I am sorry and I am concerned that the trip is too hard for you and our son. I think we will both be very dirty when we get there. It may take many baths to get us clean . . ."

Chapter 14

Pulling him against her, she kissed him. "Husband, I think you are feeling much better . . ." A week after the surgery José began walking with crutches. The trip home had been long and dusty but otherwise safe. His foot hurt badly for the first week. After he took the stitches out; Sara Song cleaned the wound twice a day and applied her aloe medicine to it.

Sheriff Davis came by the day after he returned home, and José told him the whole story. "The Indian is smart. I was not paying enough attention and he almost killed me."

"How bad do you think he's hurt?"

"I think he might have a damaged left hand, but nothing worse."

"I will make up a new warrant and add this to the charges then I'll send one to every county in the territory as well as Texas and eastern Arizona. Someone may find him."

"No one will find him."

"José, you won't be ready to go out for quite a while."

"No one else can find him. When I can ride, I will find him, this needs to be finished."

"Okay José. Just let me know when you are ready," said Davis. "I'll let you know if I hear anything about him."

José practiced for several days with crutches until he could put weight on his foot. For the next week, he walked with a cane that Albert had made for him from a twisted piece of mesquite. After two weeks, he could mount a horse from the right side, though his left foot would not fit in the stirrup without considerable pain.

José sat on the bed in front of the fire while Sara Song rubbed his foot with her cream. He caressed her belly, now showing large with the baby. "Husband, please do not go looking for the outlaw Indian again. Soon we will have a child and we will need you here."

"I promise you I will not go until our child is born. My foot should be good by then."

While he was healing, he spent time watching Albert and Isaac work the young horses in the round pen. "Soon, huh boss?" asked Isaac.

"Soon?"

"The baby soon?"

"Yes, the baby, very soon Isaac."

"Boss, I have something to ask you please."

"What is it?"

"I have found a woman to be my wife, her name is Marie. When we get married I want her to live with me in the cabin." José put out his hand to the young man. "Congratulations Isaac, bring her to the cabin and she will be part of our family."

"Thank you boss, we will be married soon at her father's house and return to the cabin."

"Isaac, when you are ready, pick a horse for each of you as my gift. If you need anything else, or need to enlarge the cabin, we can do that too."

Isaac thanked him again and embraced him tightly. "You are welcome," said José, pushing back slightly. It was the first time a man ever embraced him like that.

*

The baby came in the fall. A boy, just as José predicted. Laura and two women from neighboring ranches helped with the delivery. He worked in the barn while he waited for word on the baby. By late afternoon he was beginning to get frustrated with waiting.

"It's okay boss," said Albert. "These things can take a while. Laura will let you know when the baby is here."

For the next hour, he busied himself with his log book of horse sales and breeding information. He heard the door of the cabin bang and turned to see Laura walking toward him. "Mister

135

José, it is time to come and see the newest member of your family."

He walked with her to the cabin, still leaning heavily on his cane. "Is my wife okay?"

"She is well."

"Is my son okay?"

"How do you know it is a boy?" asked Laura.

"It is. He is okay?"

Laura nodded. "They are both well."

Walking into the cabin, he heard his new son crying before he saw him. Sara Song put him to her breast and began to feed him.

"Our son is hungry, that is a good sign."

Sitting on the bed next to her, he stroked her hair and kissed her gently. "Husband, you can touch our son, he will not mind."

He reached out slowly and touched the baby's hair. It was thick and black, more than he had ever seen on a baby before.

"Husband, we have a beautiful son, just like you said. We must give him a name. Have you thought about this?"

"I think we will sleep tonight and make a name for him tomorrow."

In the morning, she handed the baby to José and he held him for the first time. "Take him in your arms, he is not like a hen's egg, you will not break him."

José held the baby wrapped in a beautiful Navajo blanket with his face just peeking out at him. "John. I will name him John. My father was Mexican and my mother was Chinese. When they came to the territory from El Paso, he chose a new family name because he wanted to sound more American. He chose Taylor. I want our son to have an American first name too."

She nodded. "Then it will be John Taylor. It seems to be important for many Americans to have three names. I like this name; it is from the book that Laura has been reading to me."

He looked at the book. "This one . . ." She was pointing at the name, *Kenneth,* the first name of the author. "Husband, I like this name. It sounds very dignified and official."

He bent down and stroked the baby's hair again. "John Kenneth Taylor, meet your mother and father, Sara Song and José Taylor . . ."

After several weeks his surgery was well healed, but riding or walking on it still gave him pain. He put more padding in the oversized boot but the heel still hurt. "You're not as young as you used to be," the local doctor told him. "It just takes time Mister Taylor. Your surgeon must have told you it may never be pain free?"

"He did. After all these weeks, I was hoping for more."

"It's just the way it is. Have your wife help you keep it clean and continue to apply the aloe, it's the best thing you can do."

José stopped to visit with the sheriff before he left. Still using his cane, he walked over to the desk and sat down. "Have you heard anything about the Indian ?"

"Nothing. Maybe you did kill him?"

José shook his head. "He is not dead. I will find him when I return from Colorado."

"You're going to Colorado? How long will you be gone?"

"Perhaps two weeks. If I finish my business sooner, I will return then."

"Are you taking Sara Song and the baby?"

"Yes. I would like to know if you will check on Albert and Laura when I'm gone? Also, Isaac and his new wife Marie live in the cabin in the back. They know how to run the ranch, but I would like you to check on them every few days."

"I'll be happy to do that."

That night at supper José announced that he, Sara Song and baby John were going to Colorado to see the property he bought several years ago. "We will leave in two days on the train to Colorado Springs, then another to Fairplay. I wired the sheriff of Park County and asked him to reserve a room for us in the local hotel."

"Husband, I have never been on a train. Will the trip be difficult?"

"The trip is much easier than on horses or in wagons. You and John will do well. In a few days you will see our new home."

"We are ready for an adventure," she said, kissing baby John on the forehead.

*

As the train built up steam, they found seats in the back of the first car. José had Sara Song sit against the window and he took the aisle seat. She built a small pallet in between for the baby. When the train started to lurch forward she grabbed for something as it began to pick up speed she gathered up the baby and looked at José. "Husband, what is happening?"

"It is just the way of the train. It takes time to start up, it will be okay."

When the train reached speed, the conductor, dressed in a clean blue suit and hat with a gold badge on it, came down the aisle carrying a stick with a small brass hook on the end. Reaching up, he used it to open the overhead transom windows. When he was done, he opened some of the windows next to the empty seats. Finishing this, he pulled out a small bag and started collecting tickets. When he reached José, he stopped and stared at him. "Tickets please."

José handed him their tickets.

The conductor punched a small hole in each one and handed them back. "Señor, you look very much like Andres Taylor, the station master in Magdalena."

"He is my brother; we look much alike."

"You are José Taylor the lawman?"

"I am."

"I am happy to meet you. Andres talks about you often. You have a beautiful family. Please let me know if I can do anything for you."

"And your name is?"

"Fidel."

"Thank you Fidel ."

Sara Song quickly became used to the sway and jerk of the car and the clacking of the wheels as the train sped across the prairie. Baby John slept through most of the trip, waking up just long enough to feed and falling back asleep when finished. Changing to the northbound train in Socorro, José held the baby while they climbed aboard. Finding a seat, they settled in for the ride to Colorado. This conductor, a very tall white man, punched their tickets without speaking.

The train from Magdalena, carried mostly working people and cars full of livestock. This passenger car was much nicer, filled with white men in good clothes and starched white collars and women in long dresses and large hats. Several stared at José and his family without speaking. The couple in the seat across from them got up and moved to another seat farther forward. Several other people moved to the next car.

"Husband, is there something happening here that I am not understanding?"

"Some people do not like to be around Mexicans or Indians, it is just their way. Pay them no attention."

After a very long ride and a train change in Albuquerque, the train reached Raton. It stopped for water and coal and to board a few passengers then began the long pull up the pass. When they crested the summit, they were in Colorado and they began the short downhill run into Trinidad. At the station, they stopped for the passengers and freight. Within an hour they were heading north again. The next stop was Pueblo, then Colorado Springs.

They watched herds of pronghorn antelope feeding on the flats and racing the train as they rolled along the foothills. By the time they reached Colorado Springs, they were both ready for a good meal and a bed.

They were met by El Paso County Sheriff Sheldon Monroe. "Good to meet you deputy," said Monroe. "I've heard a lot about you over the years, it's nice to finally meet you in person."

"You know who I am here in Colorado?" asked José.

"Sure do. Everyone here has heard about your work. They would all like to meet you."

"That will be okay, but do you know where I can get a room? My wife and son need a place to rest."

"Already taken care of. You will be staying at General Palmer's new hotel called the Antlers, the finest hotel in Southern Colorado."

"How did you know I was coming?"

"Sheriff Davis wired me and asked me to take good care of you and your family."

"Thank you. I didn't know that he was going to do that."

"Let's get you into the hotel so your family can freshen up. We can have a good meal and a drink when you're ready."

"Thank you. Who is General Palmer?"

"You are going to meet him tonight. He's the king of Colorado, at least as far as most people around here think. He's an ex-soldier that came West to seek his fortune and ended up the founder of Colorado Springs. The man has built railroads all over the West, great hotels and a large part of this city."

The room on the second floor had a balcony looking straight out at Pikes Peak, the mountain named for one of the first white explorer's in the area. "Husband, is this where we are going to live?"

José shook his head. "We will live on the other side of that mountain. Tomorrow we will take a shorter train ride to Fairplay.

That is where our land is? This is a beautiful place."

"You will like the other place even more," said José. "The closest town to our land is very small, it will be a good place for our children."

The meal was served in their room, then Sara Song and baby John retired for the night. Sheriff Monroe walked with José to the bar and introduced him to several men. "Barkeep, set up my friend here with the finest whisky in the house."

"No thank you," said José. "I do not drink whisky; it makes men do dumb things."

"It can do that for sure," said Monroe. "How about a beer instead?"

"That will be okay. Why did you have our meals served in our room? "

"Uh . . . well, I just thought the trip had been long and tiring and it would be easier on your family."

Before he could answer, a slim, distinguished looking man with fine graying hair and a bushy mustache, walked up to their table and said hello. "José, this is General William J. Palmer," said Monroe.

He put out his hand and Palmer shook it vigorously. "The sheriff has told me a lot about you. He said you are one of the toughest lawmen in the country. He says that you can find anyone and always bring in your man. That right?"

"No sir, I do not get all of them . . ."

Ignoring the comment, Palmer continued. "I am looking for a detective to take care of security for my railroads, you interested in the job?"

"Thank you for the offer sir, but I am about to retire from this job and take up ranching in South Park. I have already purchased the land."

"Fair enough," said Palmer. "I'm disappointed, but if you ever need a job in the future you will think about working for me?"

José nodded. "I will think about it."

Palmer shook his hand again and walked away. "He's a good man to work for, José."

"I have already made my plans."

"Well, hope it works out for you and your family. When you head up to Fairplay, you will be riding on his train. At the town of Divide there's also a line to Cripple Creek, you might want to visit there before you leave."

"I will remember that."

The train pulled hard up Ute pass and swayed and jerked its way to the top. It twisted and turned through steep canyons lined with red granite walls. The line followed a small creek flowing down through the village of Woodland Park. Winding through the hills, it dropped down into a place called South Park. "Wife, this is our new home."

"All of this is our land?"

"No, we will live against those tall white mountains you see. We have one section of ground to start. We will raise horses and cattle."

"Is there a place for us to live?"

"Not yet."

The train pulled into the tiny Fairplay station and José helped her climb down from the train with the baby in her arms. Standing on the platform, she looked at the snow-covered peaks of the Mosquito Mountains and their tree covered flanks. "Husband, this place is beautiful, you did well to find it. We will like living here."

After a day's rest at the town hotel, a buckboard met him in front. The driver was a local named Deacon Roberts. "Mister Roberts, what is it that you do here?" asked Sara Song.

"Call me Deacon please. I am a rancher and a builder, Missus Taylor. I do just about anything there is to do on a ranch. My ground is next to your husband's."

"I asked him to go with us today to talk about some things at our new home," said José. "I want to have some work done before we return so we will have a place to keep our horses when we bring them back."

"And a house for us?"

"We will build it when we get here in the spring."

"Husband, we have baby John now, where will we sleep while we are building it?"

"For a while we will stay in the hotel. When it is warm enough, we will set a tent on the property so I can work on it every day."

She frowned slightly. "We will miss our beautiful warm cabin. I hope you can build it quickly."

"Do not worry wife, you know I will always take care of you and John."

After a short ride, the wagon stopped in front of a small cabin with several horses and cows in a pen behind it. "This is my place," said Roberts. "The south side of my property is the north side of yours. Do you want to take a walk around it right now? Your wife and baby can visit with my wife inside the cabin if you would like."

The two men walked the property, and José laid out the spot for the barn. "I want you to build a barn right here," said José, scratching a line in the dirt with his cane. "It will need to have eight stalls, four on each side, a common area on this end and a good loft. Outside of the other end I want a pen about 50 yards square. Can you have this ready by April?"

"Yessir. I have three strong sons that work with me, we can do this. What about the cabin?"

"I will build it myself. It will be twenty foot by forty foot. I want it to look out on the valley and set just below that big rimrock ridge. Also, I would like to have more than enough logs on the site, already peeled and ready to work with."

"We can do this. I have a small timber business also. We can also provide you with some stone from my property for your fireplace if you need it. And we will be here if you need any help."

"Thank you. The creek in back, has it ever stopped running?"

"No, it comes from a good spring in the high country behind us. It is very good water."

"I would also like a ditch with a gate to supply water to a tank at my barn. What would it cost to have all this done by April first?"

"What about other fencing?" asked Roberts. "If you don't fence between your land and the government forest and your animals get loose, you'll play hell finding them up there."

This was one thing he hadn't planned for. "Has that happened to you before?"

"Me, and everyone else around here, many times."

"Okay. Build a four-wire fence across the back with a large gate into the forest just across from the barn. What will all this cost?"

Roberts made a few calculations on his pad and showed him the total. "This is okay. I can pay you now if you want."

"Mister Taylor, you are my new friend and neighbor. If you give me half now and half when you return in April, that will be sufficient."

José put out his hand and the men sealed the deal.

"Husband, this is a beautiful place you chose. When will we return?"

"We will move our stock up here in April. When the cabin is finished, we will return home one more time to get the rest of our possessions and dispose of the ranch."

Shaking hands with Roberts, he handed him a pouch with the first payment. I will see you in April. I have set up an account at the local bank and put some money on deposit. If you need more money or anything else, wire me at the Magdalena Sheriff's Office and they will contact me. Stepping up into the railcar he found Sara Song and the baby and slid in next to them. "Wife, you like our new home?"

"Yes, I like this place very much. But I think it may be a cold place when the snow falls."

"I think it will be better than the heat and the dust at our ranch. I think it will be a very good place to make our life and grow our children."

She put baby John to her breast and kissed José. "Thank you husband."

They were quiet all the way to Colorado Springs, enjoying the scenery and witnessing a sudden thunderstorm that blew across the flats of South Park with brilliant flashes of lightning and a heavy rain storm. Before they got across the park, the skies were blue and the storm was gone, leaving a beautiful rainbow in its place.

A special place, thought Sara Song.

Stepping off the train in Colorado Springs, they made their way to the small café in the station. Sitting near the window, they ate their meal and watched the passengers come and go. There were many more people in Colorado Springs than she had ever seen. "Husband, I never saw so many people in one place before." "Many of them are here because of the gold mining in Cripple Creek. They have come hoping they can find gold and become wealthy."

"Do they all become wealthy?"

"No. Most work for the people that own the mines. It is very dangerous and dirty work for only a few dollars."

When the southbound train blew its whistle, they sat down and prepared for the next part of the trip. By the time they reached Trinidad, it was well past dark and baby John was fussy. José found a room for the night at the Pronghorn Roadhouse at the foot of the pass and they went into the bar for a meal. They would take the first train out in the morning.

The café was a long room with a bar along one side and a dozen scattered tables and chairs. A line of men were leaning into the bar drinking and smoking. Several tables had men eating steak and potatoes. All eyes followed them as they walked to the back of the room and sat down.

When the waitress appeared, José asked what they had for supper. "We got beefsteak and plenty of potatoes. I think we have some bread if it ain't all gone already. And all we have to drink is beer or whisky."

"Do you have any fresh water?"

The waitress rolled her eyes and shook her head. "I just said all we had was beer and whisky."

"We will take two steaks, two potatoes and two beers."

The waitress walked away without responding. "Husband, I do not like this place. It does not feel right for baby John."

"We will be here long enough to eat and that is all. It will be okay."

The waitress brought the food and the beers, setting them down without speaking and left. "The beef is very burned and the potato is raw," said Sara Song.

"Mine is also bad. I will talk with the waitress." José walked to the bar and spoke to the waitress, now busy wiping it down. "Our food is not good. We would like a properly cooked meal."

"That meal is all you get. And don't think of not paying. Didn't you see the sign when you came in?"

José read the small, dirty sign above the bar:

Absolutely NO Indians Allowed!

"I do not care what the sign says. You have already served us. We will not eat this food and you will prepare us fresh meals."

"And what if she don't?" José turned to see a very tall, heavy man with a trail of tobacco juice down his shirt and a pistol in his waistband.

"My business is with her, not you."

"Little man, your business is with whoever I say it's with," said the stranger, pushing him against the bar. "Now pay the lady and get that filthy, stinkin' squaw and your half-breed out of here."

José's eyes were locked onto his. "You will apologize to my wife then you will leave. You have one minute."

"And if I don't?"

"I will put a bullet through your heart."

The stranger felt something hard against his chest. Looking down he saw a cocked Colt pistol pressing against his chest. "Who the hell are you?"

He pulled back his coat and revealed his badge. "I am Deputy Sheriff José Taylor. Now apologize to my wife or I will kill you."

The man walked slowly to the table and looked down at her and the baby. "I'm sorry lady."

In a flash, José hit him in the face with his pistol butt, causing a trickle of blood to run down across his eye. "When you talk to my wife you will remove your hat and apologize properly — do it again."

The cowboy took off his hat and held it to his chest.

"Ma'am, I am very sorry for those things I said. I hope you can forgive me."

She stared at the man saying nothing. José raised the Colt up to his chin and looked him in the eyes again as he pulled the man's pistol from his waistband. "If I ever see you again — I will kill you."

After the man left, José unloaded the pistol and set it on the bar, dropping the cartridges in the spittoon. Then he turned to the waitress. "We will have a properly cooked meal now."

"Yessir, I will get it right away."

José looked around the room, now completely quiet. The rest of the men in the bar had observed the confrontation and turned away, minding their own business.

"Husband, I thought you liked your beef burned?"

"I do."

The waitress set two fresh meals on the table and two mugs of beer. "How much is the bill?"

"No charge sir, it is on the house."

"I asked you how much is the bill . . ."

"Two dollars sir."

"Thank you."

"Husband, I have seen many men like this before. They are bad people, but you wouldn't really kill him, would you?"

"Finish your meal. We will have a good rest tonight and a long ride home tomorrow."

He dropped the money on the table and they walked to the door. Opening it slowly, he walked out and scanned the street before she stepped out with the baby. They found their room and settled in for the night. José slept with the pistol next to his hand all night. In the morning, he bought several tamales and tortillas from a vender at the station. Waiting on a plank bench at the station, they ate their meal and watched the crowds as they waited for their train. A young boy walked up to Sara Song and stared at her for a minute. "Lady, are you a real Indian ?"

She nodded. "I am Navajo."

"Where do you live at?"

"I live in New Mexico Territory, near the town of Magdalena with my husband and son."

"Is he your husband?" asked the boy, pointing to José.

"Yes. And this is our baby, John."

A heavy woman in a big hat and a long green dress walked up and took him by the hand. "Leave these people alone."

"It is alright," said Sara Song. "He was just curious."

She roughly pulled the boy away from her. "I told you to stay away from them, she's an Indian and the baby is a half breed, we don't want them near us."

Sara Song sat silent for a minute before José noticed her tears.

"He was just an innocent boy."

"Wife, I will speak to her if you wish."

She shook her head. "No, please take me home."

Chapter 15

Stepping off the train in Magdalena, they were met by Andres. "Sad news brother," said Andres, embracing him. "Father is dead. He passed in his sleep last night."

For a moment he was silent, taking in this unexpected news. Where is he Andres?"

"He is with the undertaker."

"Take me there."

"This way." said Andres. "Marisol, take everyone to the house. We will be back soon."

The two brothers stood over the coffin looking at their father. The undertaker, an elderly man wearing a dark suit and black tie, asked if they were satisfied with his work.

"Yes, thank you," said José. "Please close it and prepare it for burial now."

"Are you familiar with my mother's grave?" asked Andres. "We would like our father next to her."

"Young man, I am familiar with your mother's grave and your father will be right alongside hers. Not only that, I knew your mother too. She was a kind and beautiful woman, loved by everyone."

Andres nodded. "Thank you. How much do we owe you for your work?"

"Twenty dollars for everything."

"Can you give him a headstone like mother's?"

"Yessir, a stone like that will be six dollars more."

José handed him the money. "Can you bury him tomorrow?"

"Yessir, tomorrow at noon."

The whole town was shut down early for the funeral. There was no room left inside the church and the rest of the crowd listened to the preacher speak through the open windows. Everyone had been touched by his kindness over the years. One of the last of the early settlers in the town, he ran the railroad station almost since it opened and handled all of the livestock shipping that came in from the driveway for years. Magdalena had grown from a dead-end rail spur to a busy and successful town with his guidance and hard work.

A dozen people eulogized Heck Taylor that afternoon. The last speaker was a tall man with an impossibly long mustache walking with a cane. His spurs rattled slightly as he walked up to the podium. He took off his hat and set it on a stool with his cane.

"My name is Chance Patton. I am ninety-one years old and I knew Heck Taylor longer than every single one of you in this room. I was here the day he arrived with his Chinese wife, Shan Shan. She was the most beautiful woman I had ever seen. I was the cow boss for the railroad shipping operation and I worked for him every day for more than thirty years."

Patton stopped for a moment to clear his throat and take a drink of water. "I was told that he was supposed to be my boss. He was just a skinny little Mexican guy and was brand new to the job. I thought I knew more than anyone else and wouldn't have any problem pushin' him around. After a few arguments, he told me it was gonna be his way of doin' things or I would be out of a job. When I said, 'what you gonna do about it little man?' He answered by poking me in the balls with a Winchester rifle and told me he was gonna blow my huevos off. We have been great friends ever since then . . ."

Everyone in the church laughed out loud at the old timer's recollection. "Today his son Andres does the job that Heck did, and still keeps the cowboys in line. His other son José is the most famous man hunter in the New Mexico Territory." He ran his hand along the casket several times. Between the tears all he could say was "rest in peace old friend."

After the service, everyone spent the rest of the day together at Andres and Marisol's house. After supper, they sat in the warmth of the fire talking of their childhood and the story of how their parents had met and immigrated to the territory. "José, the oldest son should have something of his fathers," said Andres. "This belonged to his mother, and then he gave it to our mother when they married." Andres removed a small red cloth from an old coin purse and handed it to José. Inside was a small gold coin with strange markings and uneven edges.

"I have never seen a coin like this before. Do you know what these markings mean?"

"No, Father just showed it to me recently and told me the story."

"Perhaps you should keep it, you spent more time with him than I did."

"I would like to keep his watch if that is okay. I use it at work every day. I think the coin will be a very good thing for baby John to have someday."

"Thank you. I will keep it for him. It is time for us to get back to the ranch, we have not been there for more than two weeks."

*

Riding into the ranch everything looked very good. The grass was green from much needed recent rainstorms, and the horses were taking advantage of it in the big pasture. Andres pulled the buckboard into the barn and threw the reins over the rail. The brothers embraced one more time and said their goodbyes.

"Thank you for caring for our father for so many years," said José. "I fear I was not a good son. I should have been here more often to help."

Andres shook his head and embraced him one more time. "You had an important job to do. Now you have a wife and son to care for. Everything is as it should be. Take care of the family," said Andres, climbing up on the buckboard. "Shall we see you in town soon?"

José nodded and walked to the cabin.

Everyone was in the cabin and the smell of cornbread and frijoles filled the room. Laura was slicing a thick piece of ham for the skillet and the bread was in the oven. "Husband, the cabin smells wonderful, it may take several days to eat so much food."

"That will be okay, I am always hungry. I will not go on a trip until it is all gone."

The next few days were a pleasant distraction for José. Albert and Isaac had done a good job on the ranch, and he had little serious work to do with the horses. The nights in the cabin were as good as he could remember. Good food and a warm bed with his beautiful wife were more than he had ever hoped for.

Baby John began to capture more and more of his attention, he was learning what it was to be a father. To hold his son in his arms was the highlight of his day, at night he lay between them, wrapped in the Navajo blanket.

For several days José did what he could around the ranch, his foot still bothering him. The cane Albert made for him was now a part of his everyday routine. He was still mounting his horse from the right side, but he could put his left foot in the stirrup and spur without a problem. He carried his cane in his scabbard with his rifle.

"I have to ride into town today for business," he announced one morning.

"Husband, is your foot good enough for the ride?"

"It is okay. I will not be gone long."

In town, the cattle pens were overflowing and several large flocks of sheep were just arriving on the livestock driveway. Railroad cars lined the siding waiting to be loaded and hauled to Socorro. *I imagine Andres is busy today,* thought José.

He walked in the office and sat down across from Sheriff Davis.

"José, good to see you, the foot's doin' better?"

"It is healing. Albert made me this good cane and when it bothers me I can use it. How many warrants do you have outstanding?"

"About half a dozen or so, but all of them are small stuff," said Davis puffing on his cigar. "A couple of them are people that skipped out on paying bills, a wife beater and a man that stole three goats, that sort of thing," said Davis. "Since you have decided to leave, I have a new deputy starting tomorrow. A young man named Don Rundle. I think you know his father, Duke? He has a small farm south of here a few miles."

"I know who they are. Has he done this work before?"

"No. But he's big and strong and very smart. I want to start him on this smaller stuff first. I may ask you to show him a few things before you move."

"I will do what I can to help."

"José, you should take advantage of the time to heal up a little more. You don't need to go on any of these."

For the first time, he found himself agreeing with him about staying home. "That will be okay for now. I have a few things to do before I go back out. Tell me about the Indian , have you heard anything recently?"

"Nobody has heard anything since you shot him, I think maybe you killed him."

José shook his head. "He is not dead. We will hear from him again."

"I think you need to let this go José. It's like we've talked about before. This part of the West is changing. It's not like it was all those years ago when we started out. The railroads have opened up country that very few people have ever seen before. Many of the Indians live on reservations now, and there are roads being built everywhere. I doubt we will ever see old Indian Jake again."

"We will see him again, and I will find him and bring him in."

"José, he almost killed you once, think about your family."

"What I think is that if someone does not stop him, many families will suffer. It could be mine or yours. No, I will find him and finish this."

"Well, I'll let you know if I hear anything about him. I'll get hold of you at the ranch if something comes up."

Walking into the boot store, he looked at a display of styles and colors of boots. "Can I help you Señor?"

"I need you to make me a special pair of boots. I have a sore left foot and need more room in it."

"Si, I can do that. Are you Heck Taylor's son? I believe you were here with him once with a similar problem."

"He was my father. We did get boots from you one time."

159

"I was sad to hear about his death, he was a very good man."

José nodded. "Thank you."

"Remove your boots and let me look at your feet."

Pulling off his boots and socks, the boot maker put them both flat on a piece of cardboard and drew an outline around them. "Your right foot will fit a size ten, but that left one might need something else to accommodate the bad heel."

"Can you build the left boot to have extra room? I can also wear an extra sock if I need to."

"Si, I have an idea. Come back in a week and we can see how well it works."

"Okay, I will see you in a week."

José's next stop was the dry goods store. Walking up to the counter he looked at the rows of penny candy in big jars. "What can I help you with?" asked the shopkeeper, a slim middle-aged woman with a long apron. "Would you like to buy some candy?"

"My new son is very small, but I would like to know if you have anything that he can eat?"

"Those would not be good, but I might have something he might like. I'll be right back."

José looked over the different candies and a jar of small, dark cookies while he waited.

The woman came back with a small jar full of powder and a spoon and handed it to him. "Try this and see if you like it. Just a little at first."

José touched his tongue to the powder and was surprised to taste such a delicious treat. "This is good, what is it?"

"It is just a mix of cinnamon and sugar. I often gave my children a taste when they were fussy. Just give him a little bit on your finger once in a while."

"How much do you charge for this?"

"Four cents would be good. If you bring back the empty jar for more, it will be two cents."

"And what is this red candy here?" asked José, pointing to a jar. "That is cherry flavored and very hard but not for little children."

"How much are they?"

"Two for a penny."

"I will take four."

Returning to the cabin he showed Sara Song the cinnamon and sugar for baby John. "This is good, I think he will like it."

She tasted the powder on her finger and decided it was okay for the baby. Then she held out her finger for the baby to taste it. His face lit up and he grabbed her finger for more. "Husband, we both like this very much."

Then he handed her a piece of the cherry flavored hard candy. "Tell me if you like this."

Her face lit up like little John's when she tasted how sweet it was. "Husband, I have never had anything like this before, is this all for me?"

"Yes, I have more."

"Thank you husband," she said, kissing him on the cheek. "Sweets for my sweet . . ."

*

Albert and José watched as Isaac climbed back up on the horse. He had already hit the ground twice. Before he was settled in for the third time the horse leaped forward, made a circle around the pen and reared up on his hind feet crashing down almost to his nose and kicking his hind feet up almost vertical. This time Isaac held the reins in one hand and the nightlatch in the other pulling himself down into the saddle and holding tight. Two more jumps with a big belly-roll in between couldn't get him off.

Not ready to give in to the cowboy on his back, the big stallion repeated his jump and belly-roll routine, this time trying to rub him off on the fence. One last jump and kick and he came down so hard that he collapsed in the dirt and stayed still for several seconds. Isaac let go of the nightlatch and pulled off his hat and waved it around in victory. The horse got up slowly, shook himself off and started to trot around the pen. Isaac grinned from ear to ear.

"Boss," said Albert. "I do believe we got a real deal bronc buster here."

José nodded, "That is a good thing Albert, I think you and I are getting a little old to be doing it."

Standing in the Magdalena livery, José was leaning on his cane talking horses with the owner. Neither of them noticed when a lone figure wearing a filthy duster and a black hat pulled down low walked up behind them. "Turn around slowly you sorry murderin' bastard and look me in the eye before I deliver you to the devil."

The men turned to see who was talking, neither recognized him. "Stranger, I do not know who you are," said José. "If you put that pistol down right now, I will not kill you . . ."

"My name is Alan Daniels; you know me now?"

"Yes. You are the last of the Daniel's brothers. I put Case in prison and killed Bob. I think you must be the dumbest of the brothers. If you do not put down that gun I will kill you too."

Daniel's hands were shaking and his face was red. "You son of a bitch, I'm here to kill you. Get down on your knees and beg for your life." Still shaking, Daniels put his thumb on the hammer of his revolver.

"If you are going to kill me then do it like a man. Look me in the eyes and shoot me. Don't be a coward like your brothers, just shoot me . . ."

Now standing no more than four feet apart, his hands began to shake even worse. As he tried to pull back the hammer, the muzzle of the gun shook wildly. José swung his cane at his hand and knocked the pistol into a pile of hay. Before he knew what happened, the gunman was on his knees and José was pounding him over and over with his cane.

Collapsing to the dirt in a bloody pile, he covered his head with his hands. "No more, please don't hit me again."

"Get up — now!"

"Okay, I'm gettin' up, just don't hit me anymore"

José shackled him, picked up his hat and gun, and walked him to the jail. "This is the last of the Daniels' sons, he tried to kill me at the livery."

Sheriff Davis looked at the bloodied, miserable looking man sitting in the cell. "Jesus Christ, I thought you were smart enough to stay away from all this. What's next? Your old man gonna come lookin' for trouble too?"

"No, he's not, and this one's never going to be in trouble again either," said a booming voice behind him.

Turning around, he saw a tall heavy man with a large straw hat and a long bushy mustache standing in the doorway. "Kennedy, I'm surprised to see you here," said Davis. "If Alan keeps this shit up, you're gonna run out of sons."

José had his Colt on the man the moment he walked through the door and his eyes never left him. "Vern, I brought him here to talk to you and Deputy Taylor. Instead he goes off and does this."

"He pulled a gun on José and threatened to kill him. José musta been feeling a bit generous today, he's damn lucky he ain't dead. Instead, he's lookin' at time in prison. So why did you come here again?"

"I came to talk about Case and tell you that the family won't be any trouble to anyone again, then my idiot son does this," said Daniels. "Vern, I need my son on the ranch. Millie is sick and I have to take her to Albuquerque for a while. I need him to run the ranch and I have nobody else."

"What exactly are you asking here? You want me to let him go?" Daniels nodded and took off his hat. "If you could see your way clear to do this, I give you my word that I'll keep his head so far up a cow's ass he'll never have time to give anyone any trouble again. You hear that boy?"

Alan Daniels hung his head and gave a feeble "yes father".

"Well, this is José's call, he's the only one here that knows exactly what happened, José?"

José shrugged. "If Alan pays a good fine to the county, Case keeps out of trouble while he is in jail and pays back those that he injured, it will be okay with me."

"Kennedy, one more thing," said Davis. "He stays on the ranch."

Daniels offered his hand to the sheriff. "Vern, you have my word that he will never leave the ranch and he will never pull any of this shit again — you hear me boy?" he said, looking at his youngest son.

The prisoner mumbled something that they couldn't understand and kept his head down. Daniels walked to the cell and looked at his son. "Goddamn you boy, act like a man for once in your life — stand up and look at me! Did you hear what they said?"

Looking at his father he nodded his head.

Now red in the face and spraying spittle out of his mouth, Daniels gripped the bars screaming at his son. "Speak goddamn you, or I'll come in there and beat your ass myself!"

"Yes father, I heard them and I understand."

"What else have you got to say to these two men?"

"I am sorry for what I did, I won't be any more trouble to anybody."

Daniels looked at the two lawmen next to him. "Okay Vern, José?"

"I'll write a citation for disorderly conduct and the fine is two hundred dollars," said Davis. "Pay it now and you can go."

Daniels put the money on the desk. "Vern, José, I can't thank you enough. You know if you ever need anything from me, anything at all, just ask."

When he opened the cell door, the prisoner stepped out and shook both men's hands. "Thank you for this."

As he walked to the door, José stepped nose to nose with him. "If I hear that you are causing trouble anywhere, I will come for you."

He nodded his head and stood holding his hat, waiting for his father. "Well what the hell you waiting for? Go find your goddamn horse."

"Yessir."

Davis handed him Alan's pistol. "Please give my best to Millie and tell her I hope she gets well quickly."

"I will." Daniels thanked both of them one more time then left the office. Sitting back in his chair, Davis lit a fresh cigar. "José, that was a good thing that you did, but I'm surprised you didn't shoot him."

"A man needs a son. He has lost two already, I did not want to take his last one from him."

The sheriff looked at his deputy and exhaled a large cloud of smoke. "José, tell me, how is little John doing?"

"He is very well."

Chapter 16

José walked into the store and the boot maker greeted him. "Hola señor, I have your boots ready. The leather at the heel is softer and I made the left heel a little wider to give you more room, I hope you like it."

José pulled the boot over his socks and settled his foot into it. Walking around the room, it felt very comfortable. "This is good, I like it very much."

"I am glad it works for you."

"How much do I owe you?"

"Twelve dollars."

"Here is thirty dollars, please make me a second pair like these."

"Si, señor, I will have them next week."

Several new horses had been added to the ranch recently. One stud that José had picked up in Socorro looked particularly promising. "Run that new stud into the pen, I want to check his feet."

Isaac led him into the pen with a short rope and snubbed him off on the fencepost. He was calm when he walked him out but the horse didn't like the idea of being tied to the fence. After kicking and shaking for ten minutes he settled down enough to check him. Albert lifted the feet and José checked them over. "Albert, I think it is time to clean these up. Pull the shoes and do a reset when you have time."

"Yes boss. I am teaching Isaac to do the smithing; he can do this one."

"That is good. Saddle up the bay with the white socks. I need to do a little riding today."

Standing alongside of the horse, he dropped his cane and put his left foot in the stirrup and started to raise up. The pain was still there but he managed to get on. Settling in the saddle, he spurred the bay and started across the pasture. After half an hour he rode back to the barn, climbed off and walked to the cabin carrying the cane.

Sara Song sat on the bed feeding baby John. José kissed both of them and sat down alongside. "Husband, what have you been doing today?"

"I went to see the sheriff and to pick up my new boots. They are very comfortable. Then I went for a ride with them and they worked very well."

"Does this mean that you will soon leave us for another trip?"

"Not yet. I have to find someone to buy the ranch first. When that happens, we have to make plans to move everything to Colorado. I told the sheriff that I would be at the ranch and he could get me if something serious comes up."

"You mean Indian Jake?"

"Yes, but there could be others too."

"Please lay here on the bed," she said, handing the baby to him.

"This is our son, is he not beautiful?"

José nodded. "He is a beautiful son."

"I would like to sleep for a while. You can get to know each other better."

When she woke up she was alone in the bed. José and baby John were in the main room, sitting in front of the fireplace. She watched as José stroked his son's hair with his right hand and the baby held onto the fingers of his left. In the soft flicker of the firelight, Sara Song saw a gentleness in him she'd never seen before.

José realized just how much his life was changing. "Wife, come sit with us."

She sat down next to him and watched as the baby played with his fingers. "I have made a decision. I am selling the ranch to Albert and Isaac. They will put the payments in the bank each month. They want to raise horses and start a cattle operation, and Isaac and Marie want to start their own family."

"Husband, that would be a very good thing. Laura and Albert will have a good home for the rest of their life."

"I will deliver the horses to Colorado early in April. I will return for you and baby John as soon as I am done. Then we will all move together to our new home."

"Will you still be a deputy?"

"I will retire when I return for you and John."

"It is a long time until spring, can you not stay on the ranch?"

"I will stay and work here until I am needed by the sheriff."

She took the baby and put him to her breast. "He is hungry now. You know that I worry you are going to get shot by an outlaw again. Why must you put yourself in such danger?"

"I am a deputy sheriff; it is my job."

For two weeks the men worked the young horses as the first chill breezes of fall blew across the ranch. José always liked these kind of days, just cool enough to keep the bugs away and require a light coat.

He noticed a rider getting close to the barn, it was Sheriff Davis. Tying up, he walked over to José. "How's the foot doing?"

"It is okay to ride with; you have a job for me?"

"Yeah, if you're ready for it."

"I am ready, what is it?"

"I need you to bring this guy in. He's been stealing cattle off the driveway for a couple of months, just one or two here and there. Last week he was spotted by one of the cowboys riding drag for old man Clinton's outfit. He started shootin' at the cowboy and they took up the chase but they lost him."

"Do they think it is the Indian ?"

Davis shook his head. "They're sure he's part of a group of rustlers that call themselves the Archer County Gang out of Texas. Most of them have been caught or killed over the last year or two, except this one."

"Do you have the paperwork?"

He handed him the warrant. "Don't have a picture of this guy though. You sure you're up for this?" José nodded as he looked at the paperwork.

*

WANTED:

__Sam Jenkins:__ AKA – Skunk Jenkins - multiple warrants for cattle theft, horse theft and attempted murder. White - 39 years old – 5' 9" tall – 190 pounds – very long, dark hair
silver spurs with large rowels
Considered armed and dangerous
Recover subject dead or alive
deliver subject to Socorro County jail - Magdalena office

*

"How far up the driveway did they see him?"

"Right at the point where the trail splits to Springerville."

"I will leave in the morning. Check in at the ranch in a couple of days?"

"You know I will."

José pulled up his collar and pulled his hat down tight. Clouds had moved in and a light drizzle started to blow in his face. "Come in and get warm, no need to ride back in this weather." By the time they got to the cabin, their clothes were covered by a thin sheet of ice.

Opening the door, they felt the rush of warm air escaping the cabin. "Laura, can you make us some coffee?"

"Sure can Mister José. Sheriff Davis, good to see you again."

"Thank you ma'am," said Davis removing his hat. "Might be a bad one tonight."

"We got plenty of frijoles and coffee and lots of firewood. Just as well stay here tonight and stay warm . . ."

"Thank you again ma'am."

Sitting down in front of the fire, the two men talked business for a while. "Sheriff, welcome to our home," said Sara Song.

"Have you met our new son John?"

"I don't believe so."

She sat down between the men. "This is John Kenneth Taylor."

Laura brought them each a cup of coffee and set them on the hearth. "Supper will be ready soon."

"He's a beautiful son, you are very fortunate to have such a wonderful family."

Holding a steaming hot cup of coffee, José looked out the window at the falling snow. "I do not think we will go very far this morning. I will leave when the sun comes out and dries things up. Sheriff, you should plan on staying a while too."

"I'll have some of Laura's coffee and that wonderful ham I smell cookin'. It should be clear by then."

"We can ride back to town together when this quits."

By noon the snow had stopped and the sun came out. As things began to melt, they went to the barn and saddled up. José walked back to the cabin and put his arm around Sara Song and the baby. "This should not take very long, maybe a few days. I will stay with Andres tonight and start out in the morning."

She hugged him tightly. "Husband, please make this your last trip, we need you with us, we love you."

"I love you too. I promise not to get shot this time."

Andres and José sat at the table eating a steak fresh from the skillet. "You are moving to Colorado in the spring? Why would you leave Magdalena?"

"I want to raise horses and cattle in the mountains where it is cooler. I want my son John to be raised somewhere that is not a hot, barren desert."

"You will sell your ranch? Who can afford to buy it?"

"I am selling it to Albert and Isaac. They will make the payments to the bank in town."

"Well, if that is what you are going to do then I wish you the best of luck. You are taking your horses to Colorado too?"

"I will put them on the train and take them there in April, then return for Sara Song and John."

Andres refilled their coffee mugs and shook his head. "I am sad that you are leaving brother, but we all must do what is right for ourselves. Where are you going today?"

"I have to find a cattle thief somewhere out where the driveway splits off."

"And your foot? It is okay to travel on a horse?"

He nodded and stood up from the chair, using his cane for balance. "I will be okay, just a bit slower getting on and off the horse." "Then we will see you when you return, be safe."

The first night on the trail he camped under a cluster of cottonwoods. After finishing up some canned beans and dried deer meat, he lay back on his blanket and watched the fire burn down. It was the first time he ever brought canned food on the trail before and he thought the frijoles were very good. Laying his head on the saddle, he settled in for the night. The local coyotes serenaded him until he fell asleep. In the morning, he woke up with a start to see a pair of coyotes across from the fire pit fighting over the empty tin. Using his cane to help him stand they ignored him. He threw several rocks at them before they even looked his way. "Get on out of here, I have nothing for you." After several more rocks, the largest one grabbed the can and ran off with the other one right behind him.

At the branch to Springerville he ran into a small herd of cattle coming up from the south. José spotted the cow boss, a man he had worked with years before. "José, you out chasin' outlaws today?"

"I am. Have you lost any cattle recently?"

"Yeah, but not this trip. I started just north of Reserve, but I put on a couple of extra hands this time. Keepin' the herd as tight as I can. Plus, they're all packin' guns."

"Have you seen this thief yet?"

He shook his head. "We just found tracks. I think he just takes one or two each time. I can't spare any hands to go after him. I hear he's been spending more time down around Apache Creek or somewhere near the ruins of the old fort at Tularosa, you know that place?"

"I know it. Thank you for the information."

Heading south, he thought about the last time he chased Indian Jake through this country. This time, instead of spending days riding through the hills looking for sign, he would ride directly to the remains of the old fort and see if he could find any evidence there. After a day or two he would start working his way back toward the split in the driveway.

Reaching the stones of the abandoned fort, he picketed his horse and set up his camp several hundred yards back in the trees. By the time he had the fire going the snow and sleet started coming down in heavy waves. Putting a long rope on his horse, he tied the other end to a large piece of a dead branch. Dragging the branch would keep him from going too far while he was looking for shelter from the storm. Sliding under the branches of the largest pine he could find; he pulled his gear in with him.

Starting a small fire, he opened another tin, this time it was yellow peaches. As the storm got worse, he covered himself with his blanket and slicker and settled in for a long cold night.

When he woke up it was completely black. With his cane, he poked at the bottom branches until a narrow shaft of light penetrated the darkness. Throwing a handful of needles and twigs together he restarted his fire just enough to light up the snow cave and collect his gear. He could see blue sky above and kept poking at the branches until he had an opening big enough to crawl out of. He was greeted with a brilliant blue sky and two feet of drifted snow. His horse stood a hundred feet away belly deep in the drift with snow melting off of him.

Outside he started a larger fire then ran a rope from tree to tree and hung his saddle blanket and slicker over it. He tied the horse between the rope and the fire letting the heat and smoke blow across him. As he was warming his hands, two rabbits ran out of the opening under the tree and into the nearby rocks. "Glad I could keep you warm," said José.

After several hours, he had everything packed up and was ready to continue the search. The snow was hard to maneuver in, but if he could get to a high place to look, any tracks that he saw would be fresh. As the snow started to melt rapidly the low spots became wet and muddy and it was slow going. Several ridges and hills later he saw horse tracks and started to follow them. Soon they turned downhill and after a few more miles he heard the faint sound of cattle bawling. Looking across a marshy field, he could see several cows in a small rock enclosure with a wire gate across one end.

Crawling closer he counted eight head behind the walls. A canvas teepee sat in the trees alongside the pen and a small stack of firewood sat alongside. It looked like the cattle thief was starting his own herd at the expense of others. Returning to his horse, José found a dry spot in the thick of the trees a quarter mile from the pen and set a small camp to wait for the rustler to come back.

There was no sign of him the first day and the snow around his camp was melting quickly. The afternoon of the second day a rider leading a cow on a rope appeared out of the trees, rode up to the pen, dismounted and turned the steer and the horse into the pen. José watched the man as he started a fire. Returning to his own horse, he packed up his gear and waited in the trees until he saw the cowboy put a skillet on the fire.

José could see he was unarmed except for the rifle leaning against the rock wall. When he stepped into his tent José rode up to the rock pen, dismounted and hollered out. "Hello in the tent, someone in there?"

A man with long brown hair stuck his head out and looked at José. "Who the hell are you?"

"I am José. I just wondered if I might share your fire for a few minutes? I have some coffee and elk jerky . . ."

The long-haired cowboy, now standing outside the tent realized that the stranger's horse was standing between him and his rifle. "Okay, sure, I guess so . . ."

José never took his eyes off the outlaw. Pulling out the coffee and jerky he walked to the fire. "What is your name friend?"

The man hesitated at first. "Sam."

"Good to meet you Sam. Do you have a pot for the coffee? I have been cold all day, this will warm both of us up."

Filling a small pot from his canteen he handed it to José. "What brings you way out here?"

"I had some business down here, now I am headed back to the town of Magdalena."

"What kind of business?"

"I came looking for an outlaw, a cattle rustler."

The man stared at José, his hands starting to shake slightly. "Did you have any luck?"

"Not until now."

"What do you mean, you think I'm your rustler?"

"I know you are Sam Jenkins. You have long brown hair and spurs with big shiny rowels and I have a warrant for your arrest."

Jenkins sat down and slumped back on the ground. "Just who are you again?"

"I am Deputy Sheriff José Taylor."

"Well shit, what now?"

"I will take you and the cattle back. You will go to trial, they will find you guilty, then they will hang you."

"Is there any way I can get you to let me out of this? You can take the cattle back and you will never see me again."

"No."

"I have a little money. What if you took the cows and the money for yourself?"

"No," said José, tossing a pair of shackles to him. "Put these on, then have some coffee and jerky."

After the meal, he had the prisoner bring his saddle into the tent and set it alongside his own. Changing the shackles to behind his back, he took out a second pair and hooked one end to the saddle and one to Jenkins' left wrist. "Now take off your boots." Shoving them under his saddle, he laid back with his rifle pointed at the rustler. "Go to sleep, we have a long day tomorrow."

"I can't sleep like this . . ."

José didn't answer.

*

Washing down a few stale biscuits with several cups of coffee they broke camp, mounted up and opened the gate. Jenkins was shackled at the wrists but could still ride, working to keep the small herd in line. Pushing out the cattle, they began to move toward the trail.

"Deputy, you're pretty trusting that I won't try to run."

"If you run, I will kill you."

After a day on the trail they caught up with a larger herd being moved to Magdalena by eight cowboys. After a few minutes of conversation with the boss, José told his prisoner to move the cows into the main herd. The cow boss agreed to take them to the railhead for him.

"Okay Sam, head out. We are going to town. I will sort out who the cattle belong to later."

When they reached town, José left both horses at the livery and walked Jenkins to the jail. Sherriff Davis pushed him into the cell, slammed the door and locked it. "Holy crap, he smells like cowshit! I see where he got his nickname. He give you much trouble?"

"No. There are nine head of cattle coming up the trail that he stole. The cow boss will put them in a separate pen until we find out who owns them."

"Good, how's the foot holdin' up?"

"It is sore, sometimes I use the cane, sometimes not. Have you been to the ranch?"

Davis nodded. "Yesterday. I gotta say, that little wife of yours is one hell of a horse woman. She rides that big mare as well as any man I ever seen."

"She learned from her stepfather; he was a horse trainer."

"You headed home right now?"

"Yes. Has there been any news about the Indian ?"

"Nothing. I think his corpse is rotting away up in the mountains somewhere."

"He is not dead. He has some help up there. Someone helped him butcher a steer and haul it off.

Chapter 17

The cool fall air was a relief to José. It was easier on the horses and his heel didn't bother him as much. He had decided to sell a few horses before he moved the family to Colorado. They chose eight head for the sale. Albert and Isaac helped him trail the extra horses to Andres' pen in town the day before the advertised sale at the livery.

Andres walked into the house just as José poured himself a cup of coffee. "José, there are two trail bosses here looking for a couple of extra horses for their remudas. Can they take a look at yours?"

"Yes, but they will have to buy them at the livery tomorrow. I told him I was bringing them to the sale."

The men checked the horses over and decided they liked what they saw. "José is well known for good horses," said Andres. "Be prepared to pay well for them."

The sale brought several hundred dollars. Before José went home, he stopped at the dry goods and bought ten cents worth of hard candy. This time he bought peppermint to go with the cherry flavor. The shopkeeper refilled his jar with cinnamon and sugar for the baby.

Walking into the cabin, Sara Song was singing softly to baby John in the rocking chair. The fire was freshly laid and the cabin was very warm. "Wife, how is my family today?"

"We are well. Baby John has been active, I think he may be ready to walk on his own legs very soon. Come and hold him for a while."

He changed places with her in the chair and took the baby in his arms. "Wife, look in my shirt pocket . . ."

She pulled out a small package wrapped in brown paper. When she opened it, she smiled and kissed him on the head.

"Sweets for my sweet . . ."

"Thank you husband, are these all for me?"

He nodded. "All for you and anyone you would like to share with."

"Husband, would you like a piece of my candy?"

"Yes please."

*

José woke up to the sound of wind screaming wildly around the cabin. Looking outside he could see nothing but darkness and snow piled against the window frame. The blowing air found every crack in the old cabin and it was cold enough to see his breath. Waking up Albert, they got fresh fires going in the fireplaces and the stove. He threw another blanket over Sara Song and baby John.

"Albert, I am going to see that Isaac and Marie are okay."

Albert shook his head. "Stay here boss, I will go."

When he was ready, José opened the door and held onto it until Albert stepped outside. The wind and snow blasted him until he managed to push the door closed. He stood with his shoulder against it and waited for Albert to return. When he heard pounding on the door he let the wind blow it open just enough for him to slip inside. "They were just starting the fire when I got there. It was bad cold in there, but they will be warm soon."

"Which horses were in the barn last night?"

"Both studs were in, as well as four mares, two colts, two geldings and the ones that belong to Marie and Isaac and me, and Fast Wind."

"It will be a long night, maybe we should make a pot of coffee?"

"Yessir, coffee sounds good. I believe we may have some fresh corn bread to go with it." Albert and José took turns keeping the fires fed during the night. As soon as it was light enough they opened the front door slowly. The snow had piled up so deeply it completely covered the entrance. Pushing through the drift he made his way to the barn. Breaking the ice from their water troughs he threw each horse a generous slice of hay and gave them fresh oats.

Isaac came into the barn to help him. "Have you seen any of the other horses yet?" asked José.

"No sir, I can't see much out into the pasture. I imagine them to be back in the trees."

"Is Marie okay?"

He nodded. "She's good, but it took some time to get warmed up last night."

"Take her to the house if you would like. We will go check on the horses in the pasture then we can all come back and have a meal and stay warm until the sun comes out."

"Thank you boss, I'll tell her."

Walking through two feet of snow, they reached the corner of the pasture and he could see the horses mixed in with the trees. Isaac counted them and came up with eleven head. "I think that is all of them boss."

The cabin smelled like coffee when José walked in. "How are the horses in the pasture?" asked Albert.

"They're all good," said José. "The trees helped protect them." The snow came back that night and continued all the next day. It was the worst winter storm anyone could remember. The family huddled together in the cabin to eat and stay warm. Baby John became the center of attention for everyone. Taking his first steps in front of the fireplace, he entertained the whole family. When he wasn't sure which person to go to, José pulled out the jar of cinnamon and sugar and showed it to him. He understood what that meant and made his way to the source of the sweets every time.

When the sun finally came the snow began to melt rapidly, turning everything into a swamp and overflowing the creek. "Wife, I fear there may be no more bathing tub after this. It may be washed away by now."

"It is okay. When we get to Colorado we will build another one facing the beautiful mountains." After several days in the cabin, she announced that she would like to take Fast Wind for a ride. "I think both of us need to stretch out our legs and feel fresh air in our faces."

José nodded, telling Albert to help her saddle up her horse. "Missy, would you like me to ride with you?"

"No, I would like to ride alone. Husband, take care of baby John, and do not give him too much from the sweets jar."

"We will be fine," said José. "Albert, you keep those horses in the pasture to build up your ranch. I won't have so many to haul to Colorado."

"Boss, if you leave us one extra mare and breed her to one of your studs before you leave, we will have enough. We have decided to make this place into a cattle operation. The remaining horses will be trained as cow horses."

"A good idea. One good cow will give you at least one calf every year. It will bring more than a young horse and is a lot less work.

Keep the horses you want and sell the rest. I will help you find some good stock if you would like."

"Thank you boss, that would be very helpful for us."

Riding into town José could see damage from the recent storm. The streets were deep with mud, broken windows were everywhere and roof shingles littered the ground. The sheriff's office had a muddy trail through the front door. José sat down and waited for him to speak as he poured each of them coffee. "I see you made it through the storm okay. Did you have much damage?"

"Just small things. It looks like the town got it worse."

"I'm getting some reports on cattle loss and building damage from all over the area."

"What about Sam Jenkins the cattle thief? I see he is still here."

"The storm made it impossible to get enough jurors together for a trial, plus nobody had heard from Judge Coker in several days. I sent someone to check on him yesterday. He's way too fat to sit in a saddle so he'll be coming in a wagon when the road is better. He said he would be ready to start at 10:00 a.m. Wednesday. Will you be here?"

"Yes. Have you heard any more about the Indian?"

"Not since the last time you asked me. I don't have much for you right now, just come for the trial Wednesday."

"I will be here."

"You still planning to move to Colorado in the spring?"

"Yes. In April if the weather is good."

"You know I will be retiring next summer. If you want the job, it's yours."

"No, when I go to Colorado I will be through with being a lawman forever. I will be a rancher, nothing more."

"I hope you do well up there. I know everyone in Socorro County will miss you."

"Thank you."

"How is that new little cowboy of yours coming along?"

"He is well. He just found his legs and he walks all around the cabin."

"Have you put him on a horse yet?"

"No, but Sara Song has taken him out several times already. I think he likes it."

"I'll see you Wednesday then. Maybe you could bring her and the baby."

José nodded. "If the weather is good I will bring them."

*

The trial was short and Sam Jenkins the rustler was convicted quickly. José was the only witness to testify, the owners of the stolen cattle were all back on ranches taking care of their own storm troubles. When the jury said guilty the judge banged his gavel repeatedly. "The jury has found the defendant guilty," said Judge Coker, taking a pull from the jug on his desk. "Vern, did the gallows make it through the storm?"

"Yessir, they're fine."

"Then go ahead and hang him, one week from right now. Case closed."

"Yes your honor, one week from today." They walked the prisoner back to the jail and locked him up.

"You gonna be here for the hanging?" asked Davis.

"No, I have seen enough men die. I prefer to be at the ranch."

"I understand. Did you bring Sara Song and baby John to town today?"

"They are with Andres and Marisol. We have to stop at the dry goods, then I will bring them by so you can visit." José looked at the prisoner in the cell. "Do you think this is right? A rustler gets hung for stealing a few steers and another one for stealing two bulls. Walter Hinton shoots another man and he gets no punishment."

"It may not be right, but we all have our job to do. Judge Coker is within the law. I can't argue with him, I can only do what I am told," said Davis. "His lawyer has a week to file an appeal for him."

"I think I am glad to be retiring soon."

"Me too," said Davis, "me too."

José spent several days looking at cattle for Albert and Isaac. They bought three pregnant older cows and three heifers to start their herd. "I would not spend any money for a bull right now," said José. "I will pay for these now and in the spring, you can arrange to get a bull from someone else."

They trailed the cattle to the ranch the same afternoon and moved them into the back pasture. "There should be enough hay for these horses and cows to last until spring," said José. "If not, you will have to purchase more. You should also choose a brand for when their calves drop."

"We already got one boss," said Albert, drawing a design in the dirt. "It's called the A slash I, for Albert and Isaac."

"It looks good. I would like one of you to help me get the horses on and off the train when I bring them to Colorado in the spring. As soon as they are in the pens at the new ranch, we will return."

"I would like to go boss, if that is okay," said Albert. "I have never seen Colorado and this will likely be my only chance."

"That will be okay. Isaac can care for the ranch and keep a watch over things until we return."

Chapter 18

The spring had brought two heifer calves and two bull calves for the A/I brand. The weather was starting to warm up and José was getting impatient to move to Colorado. "I have made arrangements to move the horses on the train next week. Albert, after we load them we will not have to move them again until Colorado Springs. Then we change trains and go to the town of Fairplay."

"I'm ready whenever you need me boss."

José swung open the gate and Isaac pushed out the remaining horses. When they reached the railroad pens, one of the cowboys opened the gate and the horses moved through the alley and into a pen next to the tracks.

"I have some business in town," said José. "When you get back, tell Sara Song I will be along soon."

Albert nodded. "We will see you back at the ranch."

Tying up at the sheriff's office, José pulled out his cane and walked in.

"José, the foot hurting today?" asked Davis.

"Yes. It got banged up some in the pen, but it will be okay."

"So you're gettin' ready to leave us?"

"I will take the horses tomorrow, and then come back for the family. I wanted you to know that I would be gone."

". . . and you would like me to check on things?" interrupted Davis.

"Yes, please. Albert will be with me so there is one less person watching over them."

"I will check on them, don't worry. Don't you have one more question you want to ask?"

"About the Indian?"

"Yes, the Indian, I haven't heard anything new on him. I think you need to let that go; we've seen the last of him."

José shrugged. "Maybe you are right, it has been a while since we heard anything."

"I believe those days are over. This part of the world is becoming more civilized now, and I for one am glad to see it. So is this your last day?"

"I would like to wait on that until I come back for the family, if that is okay with you?"

"That's fine, I'll see you then. When you get back we will talk about you retiring. You should be pleased about that."

"Are you pleased about your own retirement?" asked José.

"It can't happen soon enough. I want to spend the rest of my days at the ranch with my wife and boy."

*

José played with baby john, while Sara Song helped with the meal. From the minute he could walk, he was into everything he could touch. The first time José took him outside for a walk, he ran around checking and touching everything. When they reached the creek he immediately fell in and began to float away. All José could see were the tips of his tiny moccasins floating down the creek. Pulling him from the current he rushed him back to the cabin and undressed him in front of the fire. Even though he was cold and red, he never cried. When he was warmed up he resumed roaming the cabin touching everything he could reach.

José asked Sara Song when he would speak, so far he had been silent.

"Maybe he can't speak . . ." said Albert.

"I have heard him make sounds before."

"He will speak when it is time," said Sara Song. "Husband, when you are together you must watch him closely. Little boys want to explore everything."

"He can really run fast for such short legs," said José. "I will keep him close."

In the morning Albert and José rode to Magdalena. They loaded their saddle horses into the car with the others. Climbing into the passenger car they said goodbye to Andres and found a seat. Reaching Socorro, they were moved onto a siding until they switched to a northbound track.

"This is much better than riding a horse or a buckboard," said Albert.

José nodded. "It is also much better on my foot. There will be several stops before we cross into Colorado, you may want to try and sleep."

Albert was glued to the window watching the country go by. "This is a great adventure; I will be watching out the window for a while yet."

They had stops at Albuquerque and Santa Fe for water and coal. When they reached Trinidad, the train pulled onto a siding, giving the local wranglers time to run the horses into a large pasture alongside the train to exercise them and give them fresh food and water. José watched as they loaded them back into the car. After he paid them, he returned to the passenger car and settled in for the rest of the trip.

After short stops in Trinidad and Pueblo, the train pulled into the Colorado Springs station, they were met at the depot by Sheriff Monroe. "José, it is late, we have a room for you and your man. You can rest and have a good meal on us."

"Thank you. This is Albert, he is not my man, he is my business partner. Do we have a place for my horses?"

"Just on the west side of the station. They'll be taken good care of for the night. Your train to Fairplay is at 10:00 a.m. and they will be loaded for you then."

"Thank you. I think we will clean up and get some supper now."

"Very good. If you need anything let me know. I will be at the El Paso Club."

José and Albert walked into the Antlers Hotel and rang the bell at the desk. An older man with gold rimmed glasses and a black bow tie appeared at the counter. "Yes, can I help you?"

"I have been told that we have a room reserved for tonight."

"Your name?"

"José Taylor."

"Yes, here it is, room 204. And who is this with you?"

"This is Albert Green."

"Sir, he is a negro. We do not rent rooms to black people."

"He is with me."

Leaning closer to José, the man whispered to him. "But sir, there is only one bed in each room. Surely you must want a different accommodation?"

"José stared at the clerk for a moment. Listen to me, we will be fine with one room — will that be a problem?"

"No sir, not a problem."

"That is good. May I have my key now?"

He handed him the key and pointed them to the staircase. "Second floor about halfway down on the left."

The room had a pitcher of fresh water in the basin. A bar of soap and a washrag sat next to the basin. After shaving and washing up they walked down to the dining room and found a seat in front of the rear window looking out onto the mountains. "I gotta say boss, this sure is one pretty place."

"It is Albert, but there are too many people here for me. I want to raise our children and build our ranch up in the mountains. There are fewer people up there."

The server walked up to the table and nervously waited for them to speak. "I would like a steak, burned, potato, bread and a beer."

"I would like the same thing," said Albert, "but don't burn mine."

José watched him walk away from the table and noticed the rest of the customers looking at them. When the server returned with the beer, José stopped him before he left the table. "Can you tell me why all these people are looking at us?"

"I'm sorry sir. We typically only serve white people here. I can only assume they are not used to seeing a Mexican and a black man in here, and you are carrying a gun. We do not see that in here very often."

José looked around the room again then back at him. "We are not leaving. I carry a pistol because I am a deputy sheriff," he said, showing her his badge.

"It will be fine sir, my boss said to serve you. He does not want any trouble."

"There will be no trouble from us, we just want to have a meal."

"I understand sir."

When the meal was finished, they paid and walked out the door. All eyes in the room watched them leave. "Boss, I don't see this as a very friendly place."

"People in the big city have different ideas about these things than we do Albert."

"I think Magdalena is a big enough town for me."

"That is why I like the little town where we are moving to. It is even smaller than Magdalena."

The morning meal was met with a few stares, but no comments. At the depot, José checked all the horses and watched as they were loaded on the train car. As the train started to pull out of the station and head for the mountains, it bucked and jerked as it slowly wound its way between the steep, red granite canyons of Ute Pass. The cars temporarily filled with acrid smoke as the engine struggled to pull the load up the steep grade.

By the time they reached Divide Colorado, they were surrounded by the Rocky Mountains. "You were right," said Albert. "This place is very beautiful."

"It will be a good home for animals and kids," said José, as they watched the trees and hills pass by.

When they reached a low opening in the hills at a place called Wilkerson Pass, they made the short descent into South Park. The ride across the park was short and the train came to a stop in Fairplay by mid-afternoon. On the platform, they were met by Deacon Roberts. "Good to see you again Mister Taylor. The trip went well?"

"It did. This is my partner Albert Green."

"Albert, I'm Deacon Roberts," he said, reaching out his hand. "Good to meet you."

"How was the winter?" asked José.

"Just a typical winter, snow and cold like usual, nothing out of the ordinary. How many horses did you bring with you?"

"We have eleven horses."

"Well then, shall we get them moved to your new place?"

The three men moved the horses through town and were at the property in less than an hour. Running them into the new pen, Roberts closed it behind them. José and Albert put their saddles on the rail in the barn and José pulled out his cane. They all walked around the property looking at the work that had been done since he was last here.

"This is excellent work," said José. "The barn is exactly like I wanted it and the pens and fencing are very well done. You have even laid in a good amount of hay."

Roberts nodded. "Thank you. You see we have some creek water diverted to the horse pen?"

"Yes, it looks very good," said José, as they walked toward the cabin site.

The ground had been leveled and stacks of freshly peeled logs lay on either side of the spot ready for building. "This looks good, there should be more than enough logs to do the job."

"There's one more thing Mister Taylor, right back here."

They walked behind the tallest stack of logs to find a new privy built just into the first row of trees. "I thought you might like to have one of these when you arrived," said Roberts with a grin. "This is on me, as a thank you for trusting me to get this done while you were gone over the winter."

"Thank you for that, but I will pay for it."

"I won't take any money for it sir, it's on me."

"Okay, thank you again. I want to talk about the cabin with you.

Would you like to build it too?"

Roberts nodded. "Yessir, I could use the work. Since I just live on the next property it will be easy for me."

They went over the details of the cabin for the next hour. When the doors and windows were decided, they stepped back to look at the site. "I like that you used metal on the roof of the barn. I would like the same metal on the cabin."

"We can do that. I will place the order for the metal when I get back to town. What about the fireplace?"

"Put it in the center of the back wall and give it a good mantel."

"I have stone already stockpiled on my property, so that won't be a problem. I can get started tomorrow."

"Here is what I would like, I may not be able to do as much of the work as I thought. If you would get started, I will help all I can when I return. Is this okay for you?"

"That will be good for me. My sons and I will start in the morning."

José pulled a small leather pouch out of his pocket and handed it to him. "This is what I owe for the work already done. How much will the cabin cost?"

"I don't know for sure yet, I can wire you the cost."

"Here is two hundred dollars for you to get started. Just wire me when you need more money and I will be back soon."

Waiting for the train the next morning, José walked up to the telegraph window. "I would like to send a telegraph to the Magdalena, New Mexico Territory station."

"Yessir, please write it on this form. Put the recipient on first then your name at the end." The wire was short:

Andres, leaving Colorado, will be home soon.
—José

*

The clerk read the wire and looked up at him. "Sir, you are José Taylor?"

"I am."

"This just came moments before you walked in, Mister Taylor, it's addressed to you."

José read the wire to Albert.

José, return home at once. Sheriff Davis murdered.
—Andres

"Sir? Do you still want me to send this one?"

José dropped a few coins on the counter. "Yes."

The ride home was nearly unbearable for both of them. Both were unable to understand why anyone would do something like this. Sheriff Davis was a good man, well-known and respected by everyone in the county, he was about to retire in a few weeks. Andres was standing on the platform when the train pulled in.

"Tell me what has happened brother."

"The Sheriff was at your ranch to talk to Isaac and someone opened fire from the trees."

"Sara Song and John — they are okay?"

"Laura and the others are okay?" asked Albert

"Yes. Sara Song and the baby were here with Marisol when it happened. Everyone at the ranch is okay. The Sheriff and Isaac both returned fire but it does not look like they hit the shooter. The sheriff was hit in the chest with one bullet."

"He died protecting the family?" said José.

"Yes. I have two horses waiting for you. Sara Song and the baby are with Marisol right now."

Walking in the house, Sara Song embraced him in tears. "Husband, it is terrible. Some monster just started shooting at the ranch and Sheriff Davis has been killed."

"Isaac and the Sheriff returned fire but never got a good look at the shooter," said Andres. "Isaac got Laura and Marie into the cellar while Sheriff Davis kept shooting — that is when he was hit."

"Wife, you and John will stay here for now," said José. "Albert and I will go to the ranch and see what needs to be done. I will be back for you later."

Riding up to the cabin they could see several broken windows and where bullets had pierced the cabin door. Isaac came out to greet them carrying the rifle in the crook of his arm. Inside the cabin there were a few spots where bullets had done minor damage. "What about the animals?" asked Albert. "Did he kill any of the cattle or horses?"

Isaac shook his head. "I do not think the shooter cared about them, it looked to me that he just wanted to kill someone. If the Sheriff had not been here, he would have killed more."

"Where were you when the shooting started?" asked José.

"I was talking to him near the gate and Laura and Marie were in the garden. The first shot splintered the top of the post and he started to fire back almost instantly, but he only had his pistol. He yelled at me to get the women inside," said Isaac.

"Then he was able to reach his horse and get out his rifle."

"Is that when he was hit?"

"Not that exact moment, but while he kept up fire I was able to get the women into the cellar. We were lucky that the door was open. After they were in, I closed the door and ran back to him. He was hit before I could say anything. I kept shooting until there were no more bullets coming in. Then I grabbed the women and we went in the cabin. All three of us kept watch with a gun until the sun came up. Then I started for town and met a couple of riders about a mile out. They went back and got Deputy Rundle."

"How do we find out who did this?" asked Isaac. "Sheriff Davis was a good man and a friend to everybody."

"I already know who did this," said José, "and I will find him."

The funeral was attended by everyone in Magdalena. Ranchers from all over this part of the West rode in to pay their respects. José paid for the service and a granite headstone. Working cowboys, sheepherders and railroad workers came with their rifles and kept a close watch over the service and the burial.

José took over the temporary sheriff's job long enough for the main office in Socorro to send two experienced deputies to Magdalena. They worked with Deputy Rundle, training him on procedures and warrants and wiring the information to every law agency. When José officially retired, another deputy would be assigned to Magdalena.

José returned to the cabin with Sara Song and the baby. Albert and Isaac had made the necessary repairs to the ranch and business had started to return to normal.

"Husband, you have been very quiet since the killing. Tell me what is going on."

"I cannot wait around for something to happen. I want to be with my family but I must find him and finish this."

"Who is it that you think you have to find?"

"You know who I am speaking of."

"Is this about Indian Jake? How do you know he did this? Nobody saw anyone."

"It is the Indian. This is because I shot him the first time I went after him. Now he is back and I must find him before he kills again."

She embraced him then kissed him passionately, her tears starting to flow. "Please, husband, do not do this. There are others that can go after him. We can move to Colorado now and put this behind us."

"This will never go away just because we move to Colorado.

This is the way the Indian lives and the way he believes, he will find us wherever we are. It has to be this way. It has to be me that goes after him."

*

The ranch was back in order and José went to town every two or three days. He read every wire from all the law enforcement agencies in the territory and went over every piece of information he had on Indian Jake LaSalle. He asked that any sightings or rumors of the Indian be forwarded to him. Every cowboy, rancher and sheepherder was given a copy of the warrant and the county offered a $500 reward for his capture.

Every day he rode the hills around the ranch looking for any possible sign of a stranger in the area. One of the deputies from Socorro left after two weeks and Don Rundle was chosen to become the new sheriff whenever José officially retired.

Sara Song and baby John seldom went outside and Isaac and Albert carried their guns with them at all times. On one of his trips, José talked to a cowboy just off of a drive. He told him that someone has been killing horses recently.

"They are shooting them?"

"Yeah, we've seen several dead ones," said the cowboy.

"Whoever is doing it, they're just leavin' 'em lay on the ground to rot."

"Where did you see these dead animals?"

"I was day workin' down the south side of the Datil Mountains. A couple of different ranchers lost horses; someone shoots them just to be killing them."

Over the next few days, José heard the story repeated from other cowboys several times. The killings were getting closer to Magdalena, almost like the shooter wanted to draw attention to them.

Sitting in the office with the new deputy, José read the wire just handed to him by the telegraph operator.

To: Socorro County Deputy Sheriff José Taylor,
Magdalena office.
Four sheepherder's horses killed near Springerville cutoff,
Indian Jake LaSalle spotted twice.
From: John Casum, Springerville, Arizona

"José, I'm ready to go after him," said Rundle, "just say the word."

"No. You need to stay and deal with the business here."

"I don't understand. You said yourself that this Indian has to be stopped. I can be ready to go in twenty minutes."

"No. You will stay here; you and your new deputy will have plenty to do watching things around Magdalena. The Indian has always committed his crimes for reasons that would benefit him, like food or money. He has no reason to waste his time or cartridges killing horses and nothing else. When I hunted him before, he shot my horse out from under me but I shot him before he could kill me. He is trying to get my attention; he wants me to come after him. I think he will be heard from again soon, and possibly much closer to town."

"You don't think that we can find him somewhere out on the driveway?"

José shook his head. "That is what he wants me to do. The longer he goes without seeing me, the more frustrated he will become and the bolder he will get. He does not care about the horses or other people, just me. When he could not find me at the ranch he was angry and shot Sheriff Davis instead. He has been working the driveway for so long that he knows it well. To catch him I will have to get him to go somewhere he doesn't know as well."

"So what do we do now? Just sit around and wait?"

"For now. But I think I know a way to draw him off the driveway and away from Magdalena."

"How are you going to do that?"

"We let him know that I have left this job and will be out on a drive. He will come after me."

"Let him know? How do you do that?"

"That will be the easy part."

*

"Husband, have you changed your mind about Colorado?" said Sara Song.

"I have not changed my mind. As I said, this problem will not go away just because we move to Colorado. It is better to deal with it here, before we leave."

"I am worried for our family. If the outlaw Indian is around here something bad will happen."

"I am concerned for our family too. You can live with Andres and Marisol until we catch him if you would like. They have offered and I think it would be safer for you and John."

"No. We are a family, and we will live together like a family on the ranch. It is not proper to involve them and I do not want anyone to drive us from our home. We will just have to be more watchful."

"Then I will do what it takes to make the family and the ranch safe. You and John stay inside the cabin. I will be back in a while."

Chapter 19

After working with the new deputy for a few days, José walked to the railroad pens. He found two men he had met on the driveway who agreed to hire on as day workers and guards for the ranch. One was a tall, fair-skinned bald man with an enormous straw hat and a black eye-patch called Scotty, and an older, muscular-looking black man named Sal, riding a badly worn army saddle.

Both just came off a large drive from Arizona and were looking for work. They agreed to work the ranch with Albert and Isaac and to take shifts riding the perimeter and to watch for signs of trouble. They also gathered and cut the firewood, relieving Sara Song of the chore. Several years before, Albert and José had built a comfortable bunkhouse for day work cowboys that would come for occasional jobs.

The cowboys followed him into the cabin with their gear. "Dang, I believe this is the cleanest bunkhouse this old cowboy ever stayed in before," said Scotty, after looking the room over. "My momma's house warn't this purty."

"Glad you like it," said Albert. "My wife works extra hard to keep it nice and feeds our hands well."

"I think I'm gonna like it here Albert. Please tell your Missus how much we appreciate a good bunkhouse."

Sal shook his head approvingly. "Yessir, that goes for me too."

*

For the next week, José, Andres and Rundle quietly spread the word around town that José was retired and had taken a job as trail boss to move a herd of horses east to sell to the Army at Fort Stanton. The people in town were sad to see him go and repeated the story to their friends and family again and again until it reached the Indians living in the area. José knew that even Indian Jake didn't work alone. He had contacts around the territory that kept him informed. He knew that it wouldn't take long for word to reach him.

José had wired Colonel Woods at the fort and asked if they might be interested in purchasing twenty well broke horses for the post and he wired him back that he could always use good saddle horses.

Andres knew every rancher within a hundred miles and helped arrange for the horses to make up the string. Each rancher would be paid for their horses after the cowboys and all expenses were paid and José would take no pay for the trip. When he was sure enough time had passed to get the information to the Indian, he put up a poster at the station looking for three experienced wranglers to make the trip.

José explained everything to Sal and asked if he would help him with the horses. "Happy to Mister Taylor. I always liked workin' with horses better than cows anyways." Sal had proven to

207

be an experienced horseman and would make the trip with him as his right-hand man. Albert, Isaac and Scotty would watch after the ranch.

"Sal, you have a rifle?"

"Yessir, I got me a Winchester. It's pretty old but it still shoots straight."

"That will be good. As I said, anytime the Indian is around, things could get dangerous."

"I ain't afraid, I fought lots of Injuns . . ."

"Good. We will start out tomorrow morning and head straight for the river. And Sal, one more thing. If something happens to me, you finish the drive and see to it that everyone gets paid."

"You can count on me boss, but ain't nothin' gonna happen to you. That murderin' Injun's gonna run into a rattlesnake den if he tries anything with us."

*

That night Sara Song and José talked for a long time. When baby John fell asleep they put him in the new bed that Albert made for him. They made love for the first time in days and held each other until they fell asleep.

In the morning José dressed and went into the kitchen. "Laura, it smells very good in here. Is that your grandmother's sweet bread you are making?"

"Yes, Mister José. It has been a long time since we have had it. I wanted you to have something sweet on the trail and I want to show Sara Song how to make it."

She pulled off a piece and tried it. "Husband, this is very good. It tastes like baby John's sweets in the jar."

"I had forgotten all about it," said Laura. "My mother used to make it for father."

"Are you leaving already?"

"Yes. Everything is loaded and the horses are at Andres' pen."

"Husband, I have a question . . ."

What is it?"

"Why do you always wear black clothes and a black hat?"

José was puzzled at the question. "I have always worn clothes like these. Why do you ask that?"

"Because everyone knows you as the famous deputy that always wears black."

"So why do you concern yourself with such things?"

"Does the Indian know what you look like?"

"I suppose he does, he shot at me."

"And if you are on the trail he will be able to easily pick you out as the man he wants to kill?"

This caused him to go quiet for a minute. "Wife, that is a very good question. Not one that I had considered, thank you."

José went to the barn and approached Scotty, the new cowboy. He explained to him about the clothes and asked him if he could trade hats with him for this trip. "Sure boss, but this ol' straw is gettin' kinda wore out. Yours is a much better hat."

"This will do."

"How about a shirt? I got an extra white one that'll likely fit you."

"I have a white shirt, thank you."

"One more thing, here's a red bandanna too."

"That will be good."

Walking back into the cabin everyone smiled at the new José. "With that big hat you look like a true vaquero," said Albert.

"That will be good, no one will know it is me. This is a good plan, thank you wife."

"Husband, you should also stop shaving your face every day, that will help to conceal you."

"Another good idea, thank you." He kissed her and hugged her tightly, walking slowly to the door. "I love you and our son. Do not worry, I will be back soon and this will be over."

José and Sal met the rest of the hired hands at the station. He told them what was going on and that if anyone did not want to go, it would be okay. Nobody said anything. "Remember, the Indian is looking for me. He would not be wanting to steal branded horses, he just wants to kill me, but you never know what he might do. You all know how to trail horses. Keep them together and move slowly. You must watch everything that happens around you as well as the remuda, if you see a strange rider or fresh tracks near the herd, tell me about it."

Andres swung open the gate. "Brother, you look very different. Will this be your new look from now on?"

"We will see."

"Have a safe trip. I will check on the ranch while you are gone."

The crew moved the herd out of the pen, through the middle of town and onto the trail. It would take about three days to reach the river. "I do not think the Indian will try anything until we cross the river," said José, talking to the crew at the first stop. "Here it is so flat and wide open we can see for miles in all directions. I think he will keep his distance for a while. I also think that he would wait until the sun goes down before he rides. The night watch has to pay close attention. We will cross the river near San Antonito. Even then, it will be a couple of days before we get to the mountains."

"We will still need a guard at night," said Sal. "I will take the first shift."

José nodded. "That will be good. We will take two-hour shifts. I am in no great hurry to get to Fort Stanton, even if it takes a few extra days, so don't push them too hard. Everybody will be paid for the extra time on the trail, and you all need to carry extra water. I know where most of the water holes are between here and the fort and we will make them our stops, but it is very dry in between those places."

On the third afternoon they reached the tiny crossroads of San Antonito on the west bank of the Rio Grande. In camp that night, they had fresh steaks from a young pronghorn buck Sal had killed a few hours before. The camp settled in for the evening and the men took their turns watching over the herd.

"Pretty quiet last night boss," said Sal, pouring them both a cup of coffee. "All I heard was a couple coyotes on the prowl."

"That is good. But the rest of the trip will be a little tougher. We have a couple more days of this desert then the country turns rough."

"We're ready, these guys look like good hands. I think they will do well on the trail."

"Okay. You get things moving and I will stay back and see if I can find any signs of the Indian around the camp."

"Yessir, we'll head out right now."

Riding a large circle south for two miles he found no sign of a lone rider. Turning back, he crossed the trail of the herd and rode north checking for any sign. When he didn't find any, he returned to the drive. "About ten or twelve miles from here is a small stream that will cross the trail," said José as he rode up alongside of Sal. "It will be good for the first night."

"You want me to ride ahead and check it out?"

"No, stay with the herd for now. I don't want anyone out there alone."

After a long day of thick dust and unrelenting sun, the horses sensed the water long before the men saw it. Picking up speed, the horses raced the last hundred yards and plunged into the creek with the cowboys following.

After the riders and horses were refreshed, they set a picket line and secured them for the night. Unloading the two packhorses,

Sal started a fire and laid out the cook kit and food. "I think maybe the next time a chuckwagon would be better than packhorses on a drive like this."

"Yes, it would be. But I cannot take it everywhere I want to go. You will understand soon enough what I mean."

After finishing the last of the buck, the men sat around the fire to talk and smoke. Rolling a fresh cigarette, Sal lit up with a stick from the fire and laid his head in his saddle. "We could use some more fresh meat. If someone shoots something tomorrow, I will personally cook the best steak on the critter and throw in some frijoles and hot biscuits with the deal. You good with that boss?"

"I am okay with that, as long as it does not affect the herd," said José. "I brought two tins of peaches with us. One tin will go to the first man that brings in the meat."

"What about the other one boss?" asked one of the cowboys.

"That one is mine."

Everyone had a good laugh at that and when the fire burned down the camp grew quiet. The nightriders had a good moon to watch the horses and the night went smoothly. In the morning, the herd was moving east before the sun came up.

"Sal, I'm going to check the back trail this morning. It is slightly farther to the next water hole. It is a small spring with a couple of cottonwood trees to mark the spot. Move them out and I will catch up."

"You got it boss. Let's move them out now," hollered Sal, taking the lead.

José rode the same type pattern as the day before, checking for any sign of a lone rider following them. Finding nothing suspicious he returned to the herd.

The next morning José held back while Sal moved the herd east. He put his binoculars around his neck and began to make large circles around the campsite stopping at every high point to glass the area. When he found nothing new he caught up with them and continued with the drive. That afternoon, just before they stopped for the night, Sal and José heard a lone gunshot from the arroyo in front of them. Riding ahead they saw one of the cowboys, a man named Jess, bent down cleaning a fat mule deer doe.

"Steak tonight Jess?" asked Sal.

"Steak with peaches!"

After the meal, José walked along the string of horses, checking for any problems. They all looked good with the exception of the normal dirt and trail scratches.

In the morning, everyone chose their mount for the day and saddled up. José pulled up next to Sal. "The next water is harder to find. The trail gets faint and starts to fade away in the next few miles. You will cross a dry arroyo with a very high bank on the far side. It is the only high spot in the area. There is a wide flat marshy area about a mile south of that crossing."

"I'll find it boss, no problem."

"I'm going to do my morning search. Then I will catch up and help find the water."

After the search turned up nothing new he returned to the drive. A quick thunderstorm passed over them just long enough to help cool off the horses and keep the dust down. Several close bolts of lightning stirred up the horses and everyone worked to keep the herd tightened up and pointed down the trail.

"Any sign of the Indian ?" asked Sal.

"No, nothing."

"Maybe he ain't coming. Maybe he took a liken' to where he's at?"

"No, he is out there. He is just keeping his distance, waiting for his chance."

"When will we get to the mountains?"

"Tomorrow we will see the mountains, but it will be a long day. The trail tomorrow is difficult for men and horses."

The arroyo with the high bank came into view and they pushed into it turning south. After a short ride the ground turned damp, then muddy and they spotted a stream of water trickling out of a flat pile of rocks. An ancient ring of stones held a pool of water several feet wide and ten-feet-long with a few cattails lining the edges. The horses crowded in for their first good water in miles.

"It is still early, but I want to set camp for tonight," said José. "Everyone needs a good rest and a good meal. Do we have any of that deer left?"

Sal nodded. "Plenty for tonight boss."

"That is good. Tomorrow will be a hard day."

215

The smell of coffee and biscuits woke everyone early. While Sal cooked, everyone saddled up and made sure that the herd was ready to go. José called them together around the fire. "Today will be difficult. Not far from here is an area that is made up of black lava rock. It is about four miles wide but runs for twenty miles to the north and to the south. This area is very dangerous to get through. The rocks are sharp like a razor and are full of cactus and rattlesnakes. The trail we have to go on is just wide enough for a horse. Go slowly and carefully, I do not want to see any of our horses or cowboy's get hurt or snake bit."

"You thinking of takin' the whole string through at once?" asked Sal.

"No. We will do two at a time. Put a halter on each one, and the rider in front will lead the first horse and the second one will be tail tied to that one. When I get the first two through, I will set a picket line and will ride back for more. The second trip we will bring four pair through."

"You heard the boss," hollered Sal. "Hook up two horses and let's get moving."

José started into the lava field slowly, giving the horse his head. It patiently picked its way over and around the sharp lava, his shoes sometimes clicking against the rocks. The second horse seemed to sense the danger and followed without incident. When they came out of the lava field José set the line and tied up the pair.

Returning to the herd, he had the cowboys each hook up a pair the same way. "You have to let your horse find the way at his own pace and keep some space between you. Sal, you take the lead and I will stay here with the rest."

The four cowboys headed out, each leading their pair of horses into the lava field. Reaching the other side without trouble they tied the horses with the rest of the string and started back. As soon as they cleared the lava, José was ready to go again.

"Sal, you take the lead, I will bring up the rear."
The crew moved through tall piles of enormous black rock and wide, flat areas with long deep fractures that once flowed across the desert like water. Cholla and prickly pear cactus mixed in with the long spears of the yucca plant, reached out to poke and scratch at the horses and men. By the time they all cleared the lava, the midday sun had been reflecting off the black rock taking its toll on the men and horses.

"Where to from here boss?"

"Everyone take a break and drink plenty. The next water is about five miles straight east. It is an old sheep camp at the base of the first big hill you see. There is good water there, and there should be enough grass for two or three days. There is no need to hurry, it is very dry between here and there. Stay there and rest up until I return, but keep a good watch."

"Ain't you coming with us boss?"

"No. I am going to watch the trail for a while and see what might be coming out of the lava."

"Aw shit boss, you mean we've been leading that Injun of yours right into the lava field all this time?"

José nodded.

"Ain't there any other trails through there he could use?"

"It is a very long ride to get around the black rocks. This is the only trail through them that I ever found."

"Are you going to stay here and watch for him?"

"Yes. I think he will come through tonight."

"I don't think anybody in their proper mind would make that ride at night, it's way too dangerous."

"He will do it."

"Okay then, we'll see you at the water hole."

"If the grass runs out before I get back can you find Fort Stanton?"

"I'll find it boss."

"Once you leave the water heading east, the trail is well defined through the pass and then turns into a wagon road. It is easy from there. If you have to do this, ask for Colonel Elias Woods when you get there. Tell him what is going on."

"Colonel Elias Woods, will do. But I'm sure you will take care of business and be back soon enough."

It was midday when the herd finally disappeared from sight. José sat down and cleaned his Winchester and Colt while his horse rested in the shade of a pair of cottonwood trees. He cleaned the binoculars and strung them around his neck. As the sun began to go down he mounted up and rode to the edge of the black rock where the trail came out. Picking out a spot behind a large hill of lava off the side of the trail, he tied the horse behind it and climbed to the top.

He took a sip of water, got as comfortable as possible and watched the sun drop behind the far hills. From here, he could see down the trail for several hundred yards. The night sky was clear and the moon just bright enough to see anything that might be moving. The smell of the sage surrounded him as he waited. For three hours he remained motionless, staring at the trail.

Moving just enough to take another sip from the canteen, he saw what he thought could be a bird on the rocks. It was a long way off, but it was definitely moving. Looking through his binoculars he saw the small dark shadow disappear then reappear moments later. This went on for another twenty minutes as he stared through the binoculars hardly taking a breath. The shadow moved slowly but steadily through the lava. As he watched, it disappeared behind a tall pile of rocks, then reappeared in front of it. It was a rider picking his way silently along the trail. He was not holding his reins, he was carrying a rifle and looking straight ahead.

José watched as he turned to start into the last stretch of the trail then suddenly stopped short. His horse threw his head up in the air and caught a scent. José froze up waiting for something to happen. His rifle was pointed at the rider and the hammer was back, but it was too dark against the black rocks to see his target clearly.

Ten minutes of complete silence were broken by a shrill scream from the rider . . . "Yip yip yee lawman, I think you are there, my horse can smell you, and even he thinks you stink like a pig! I have come to kill you! You will not get away from me this time. I will kill you like I did your fat friend. I enjoyed killing him very much, and now I shall enjoy killing you too!"

The Indian's horse took a few steps closer, while he was still screaming. The rider was difficult to see, but his horse stood out well. When he got a clear look at the horse he squeezed the trigger. It dropped like a stone in the middle of the trail. When he put up his binoculars the Indian was nowhere to be seen. *Now we are both on foot, you cannot run away again,* said José to himself. He knew chasing him through the black rock would not be easy, but this time the Indian would have to stay and fight, just what he wanted.

José stripped all the tack from his horse, put on a halter and turned it out, then pushed his gear under a rocky overhang. Removing his boots, he rubbed Sara Song's cream on his sore heel and put on his clean socks. After tucking his pants into his boots, he slung both canteens over his shoulders. "Okay Indian ," he said softly, picking up his rifle, "it is time to finish this."

Sal woke up to see José's horse standing in the water with the rest of the remuda. One of the cowboys caught him and tied him to the line. "Looks like he put a halter on him before he turned him loose," said the cowboy.

Sal had already decided to move the remuda to the fort as José had instructed when he saw the horse. "I think he let him go so he could work on foot. We will go to the fort and sell the horses and return to look for him. Let's move 'em out."

Sal expertly moved the herd across the last of the desert and through the low pass in the Ruidoso Mountains and connected with the wagon road. After finding his way to Fort Stanton, he moved the horses to the pens behind the livery. "Delivery to Colonel Elias Woods from José Taylor of Magdalena."

The wrangler swung open the gate and twenty head of horses plus José's ran in and lined up at the water trough. "You'll need to see the Colonel, he's over at the quartermaster's office right now. It's the last building on the left."

"Can we put our horses in there?" asked Sal. "It's been a long dry trail."

"You bet, run 'em on in."

The cowboys stripped their horses and set their gear on the fence rail, and ran their mounts into the corral.

Sal found the Colonel engrossed in paperwork when he walked in. "Would you be Colonel Woods?"

"Yes, I'm Colonel Elias Woods, can I do something for you?"

"Yessir, my name is Sal, I work for José Taylor. I just delivered twenty head of horses to your wrangler."

"Where is José?"

"Well, sir, he stayed back at the lava field. He's trying to catch Jake LaSalle when he comes through."

"Indian Jake? That no good son of a bitch is still alive?"

"Yessir. He killed Sheriff Davis and José is hunting for him."

"Damn, I thought José killed him last fall."

"No sir, he just wounded him. Now the Indian wants his revenge."

Woods thought about this for a minute. "You say that José is in the lava field looking for Indian Jake on foot?"

Sal nodded. "It looks that way sir."

"Then we have to go find him. The last time he was here he'd been shot in the foot. Is that all healed up now?"

"He had it fixed a while back, but it still bothers him some."

"You and your hands can bunk in the barracks tonight and we will head out in the morning. I will not leave him out there by himself."

The cowboys, four soldiers and the Colonel himself headed out at first light. José's saddle horse was tied behind the wagon. When they reached the pass, they set camp for the night. "Sal, tell me what happened between José and the Indian."

"Well, sir, I don't know all the details, but the Indian had been stealing cattle along the driveway and José went lookin' for him. All I know for sure is that he got ambushed by the Indian and got his horse shot out from under him. José shot him, but he still had a horse and he ran off. José was on the ground thirty miles from nowhere and had to walk back to civilization. After several days, his bad foot gave out and he collapsed."

"Then what? How'd they find him?"

"Well, the story is that his Indian wife, a Navajo named Sara Song, went searching and tracked him down. This was more than a week after he got shot. They say he was makin' peace with his maker when she finally got to him."

"Well, goddamn, that's quite a woman he's got there."

"She is sir, and they also got a new baby boy named John."

"Sal, we ain't about to let such a good man die, we're gonna keep looking 'till we find him."

*

José lay flat on his belly nestled between two piles of lava rock with his rifle at his side and the binoculars pressed against his eyes. The sun was relentless and made the glare in the binoculars difficult to look through. Earlier the first day he caught a movement that he thought may be the Indian, but was nothing more than a few ravens. He saw a bobcat in the distance and one rattlesnake. He killed the snake with his rifle butt and cut it into three pieces, eating one piece right away and saving the rest for later.

As he crawled in and out of the cracks and around the jumbled hills of rock, he stared at every surface and plant for sign. Studying each spot of sand or dust he would move a few more yards and do it again. After each move he stopped and listened for a long time. At the bottom of the cracks were layers of fine sand carried into the lava field from years of storms. Making his way to the dead horse, he looked for anything that would point out the direction the Indian went.

Finding nothing, he made a cut down the horse's backbone, skinned the hide back and cut out a long piece of meat. Cutting it into smaller pieces he ate several and took a swallow of water. Throwing it into the pack with the rattlesnake he settled back into the sand at the bottom of the trail and listened. He sat silently as the daylight began to disappear. Just as it dropped from sight he heard the distinct sound of one rock click against another one. A minute later he heard it again. It came from the north, not close, but definitely north of where he was.

The night was overcast and traveling through the lava field in the dark was too dangerous. He lay down against the dead horse for warmth, knowing it would be a long night.

When the skies started to lighten, he ate several pieces of meat and took a swallow of water. Climbing up onto the rocks he scanned the surrounding area and began to crawl between the cactus and over the lava rock, dropping down into another wide split. This one was wider but barely two foot deep with little sand on the bottom. He wedged himself into an awkward sitting position, took another sip of water and waited.

He noticed for the first time that he had blood on his shirt and his rifle. The lava rock had badly chewed away at his clothes and skin while he crawled from place to place. His hands were covered with scratches and small cuts smeared with blood. As he sat listening, the clouds and the wind began to blow across the lava field. Within minutes the temperature dropped. Rain and sleet pounded the rocks and José pulled down his straw hat and waited to see what was next.

The storm moved fast, but left a lot of water behind. He was soaked and sitting in several inches of water by the time it blew over. When the sun came out he pulled off his boots and socks to give them a chance to dry in the heat.

Crawling out of his hole he scanned the black rock in every direction with his binoculars. He picked out a high jumble of rocks in the distance and made his way to it with his rifle across his arms. The rain had left small pools of water in the holes and depressions in the rock. He was able to get enough water to drink and enough to fill his canteen. Reaching the high spot, he worked himself to the top and scanned the area. Concealing himself the best he could he sat back and watched and listened while he finished the rattlesnake.

Two coyotes trying to catch a rabbit and a few ravens were all he had seen or heard for several hours. Shifting himself around to relieve the pressure on his heel he saw a lizard sunning itself on the rocks several feet below him. There was more life in this forbidding looking rock pile than he realized.

*

Sal stopped short of the lava field with Colonel Woods and pointed out where the trail came through. "I think he waited for the Indian right around there somewhere Colonel."

Woods spurred his horse and headed for the spot. Dismounting, he walked back and forth along the trail. "Nothing I can see here, any tracks have been washed away by rain," he said to the wagon driver. "Tie my horse to the wagon."

"Yes sir."

Woods climbed in and out of the rocks on either side of the trail looking closely at every one of them. "Sal, come here."
Under an overhang was a saddle and the rest of José's tack and extra gear. "He was okay when he put this stuff here."
Woods directed his men to find everything José had left behind and put it in the wagon. "Sal, you want to bet on which direction they went from here?"

"Couldn't really say Colonel. Maybe a couple of us should take a ride in for a ways, we might learn something there."

Woods nodded and turned his horse onto the trail. A short ways down the trail they came to the dead horse. "Hell, This is a goddamn Indian horse, just sure as I'm wearing blue!"

"Yessir, it sure is. It looks like José shot the horse out from under old Jake this time. That's why he turned his loose, he couldn't use a horse in there so he went after him on foot."

Woods nodded, looking at the cut in the back of the horse. "Looks like he took a little fresh meat with him too. Sal, this is one tough son of a bitch . . ."

"Yessir Colonel, I ain't knowed him all that long, but there are plenty of stories out there about him. They say he hunted down the man that killed his mama when he was just a kid. Shot him through the heart way down in some dusty little town called Alma and hauled his corpse all the way back to Magdalena just to show his father. They say that's also what made him such a hard case."

"I can see that," said Woods. "This is tough country; it can make you grow up fast."

"What now Colonel?"

"First let's get out of this nasty stuff. "

At the edge of the black rock, Woods climbed up on the wagon and scanned the lava flow with his binoculars. "I can't see anyone out there; the country is just too rough and broken up."

"I guess 'bout all we can do is wait here and see what happens," said Sal.

Woods pointed to his mounted soldiers. "Trooper Johnson, you and Simmons mount up and ride along the edge of the field for a couple of miles. One of you head south and one of you head north, see if you can find where someone came out."

Colonel Woods and Sal sat on the tail of the wagon looking out at the lava. "The locals call this the *Malpais*," said Woods. "It's Spanish for badlands. Not much good for anything, just a miserable waste land."

*

José moved down from the rock pile to relieve the cramps in his legs. His heel was starting to throb and he felt the need to take off his boot. Finding a suitable place to sit, he pulled off his boot and sock. The rocks around him still held a few puddles of rainwater in them and he put his foot in the largest one. It felt good to get it out of the boot, even for a few minutes. After his foot dried he rubbed the last of the aloe cream on it and pulled the boot back on.

The sun set before he could go any farther and the clouds covered the moon. It was about as dark and still as any night he could remember. Hunkering down against the rock he had a few bites of meat and drank a little water. He knew he needed some sleep and this might be his only chance so he let himself drift off with the Colt in his hand.

The call of a coyote startled him awake. It was just starting to show a sliver of morning light. José felt better than he had in the last several days. He raised up enough to use his binoculars to scan the surrounding rock. Seeing nothing out of the ordinary, he ate a little, took a swallow from the canteen and crawled back up the rock pile.

He estimated he had covered well over a mile since he left the dead horse. Staring through the binoculars he was sure that he was on the right trail. Picking another landmark, he worked his way forward, trying to avoid the cactus. He came to a long narrow strip of open ground covered in sand. Seeing nothing but a few coyote tracks, he cautiously followed the sand for several hundred yards to the edge of another high, twisted pile of yucca covered rock. Crawling up to the top he went back to scanning the area.

Immediately he saw several ravens circling around a lump of black rock. Two were on the rock pecking at something. Several other birds were diving in looking to see what it is. Deciding he needed to get a closer look, he started to crawl toward the spot and see what the birds were interested in. When he reached the place, he saw several drops of blood smeared across the rock and a tiny, bloody sliver of something stuck in the drops. He pulled it up and stared at it for a moment before it came to him what he was looking at. It was a thin piece of leather soaked in blood. He was looking at a scrap of a moccasin covered in blood. The sharp volcanic rocks had destroyed the Indian's moccasins and started to cut into his feet, he was leaving a blood trail.

Crawling to the next high point, he scanned the area looking for more blood sign. In the distance, he saw what looked like a reddish streak on a wide flat piece of rock. Remembering the last time he went after the Indian, he started to move away from the blood. Making a wide circle around the spot he started to crawl in from the opposite side. As he squinted through the binoculars the sun reflected off the lens and a bullet instantly grazed the edge of the binoculars, shattering them. José fell back on the rock with his hand over his eye. Pouring water on his face he wiped at it with his bandanna. His vision was okay, but the binoculars were destroyed.

A high-pitched voice came out from the rocks. "Hey lawman, did I kill you this time? I am the winner lawman, you died first, the ravens will soon be picking at your bones!"

Moving lower in the rocks he worked himself closer to the Indian. Reaching a clump of yucca plants, he crawled up to them and used his rifle barrel to spread them apart. He was looking directly down into another wide crack in the lava rock. The sand in the bottom had been disturbed.

Pushing the yuccas farther apart for a better look, he saw a movement in the sand. It moved again and this time he could see that it was the end of a rifle butt. He put his sight right on it, pulled back the hammer and waited.

"That you lawman? I smell something awful — like a Mexican pig — it has to be you. Tell me it is you lawman, so I know who I will kill today — then this will be over."

José spoke for the first time. "Indian, today you will not kill anyone — today is your day to die . . ."

"Lawman, you would not kill a tired old Indian who has lost his moccasins on this terrible rock would you? I am not able to walk anymore, I surrender, you can take me to jail now lawman."

José never moved; his rifle still locked on the target. "Indian If you stand like a man I will kill you quickly. If you make me come down there it will be much worse for you. Stand up now."

"Okay lawman, I will stand, but I must say a prayer before I die."

José saw the rifle butt pull back. A second later the outlaw stood straight up and charged forward, shrieking at the top of his lungs and firing his rifle from a few feet away. Just as he reached him José fired and the Indian fell back into the crack in the black rock.

Climbing down to the lifeless body. Indian Jake LaSalle lay in a twisted pile with a bullet through his heart. Both of his hands and feet were raw and bloody. His body was covered in cuts and cactus scars and covered with blood. He had used his shirt as bandages for his feet. The thumb on his right hand was missing from some long-ago injury and two of the fingers on his left hand were severely crippled. His body was little more than loose skin hanging from bones, and he had scars from bullet wounds and a long knife cut across his chest. Unable to walk, he had no food or water left but still had the strength to charge him. He gathered up his rifle and knife and looked at the lifeless corpse of his long-time adversary laying in the black rock. "Now it is over Indian."

He started walking straight east. Even when he could walk upright the terrain was difficult. After having some water and the last of the meat, he looked back to see the ravens already circling the body. For several hours he walked and climbed in and out of the lava, his foot throbbing painfully. He thought about how the Indian had spent so many years as an outlaw without being caught. He had been hunted for more than fifteen years for nearly every crime there was in the territory.

Lawmen and bounty hunters had chased him all over this part of the West for years. He fought white men and Mexicans with equal vengeance, but stories of him helping other Indians had also been repeated many times. He was likely one of the last really bad men left in this part of the West, at least in the eyes of the law.

Reaching the edge of the black rock he stepped onto the soft dirt, dropped everything and sat down. After taking several long swallows of water he fired his rifle three times. Within a few minutes he heard three returned shots. Firing three more rounds he lay back and fell asleep.

"There he is," shouted Sal, "I see him!"

Sliding to a stop, he jumped off his horse and ran to the body lying on the ground. "José, are you okay?"

Lifting the straw hat off his face, he looked up at Sal. "I am okay, just tired."

"And what of the Indian ?"

"He is dead."

Colonel Woods and his men pulled up next to them.

"Damn José, I was afraid we might have lost you out there in that wasteland."

"I am okay Colonel, thank you for coming."

"I take it that you killed that no good murderin' Injun?"

"Yes."

"Good, we will set camp here for tonight. We have plenty of food and water and you can rest up," said Woods. Looking at him closely he was surprised how rough he looked. "José, that rock really did a nasty job on you, you look to be bleeding just about everywhere. Trooper, find an extra pair of pants and a shirt for him. And bring a blanket and the medical box too."

"I am okay Colonel, really."

"You are not okay Mister Taylor, not until I say so, now lay down on the blanket."

José was too tired to argue and lay back.

"Sergeant Simmons here is our medical expert, he will attend to those wounds."

"Thank you again Colonel," said José, falling asleep almost immediately.

Waking up an hour later he sat up and looked at everyone sitting around the fire. "Did you find anything that needed attention?"

"The sergeant sewed up a couple of small wounds and pulled so many cactus needles from you that he lost count at a hundred," said Sal.

"I feel okay," said José.

"You should, he also gave you a big shot of morphine," said Woods. "That'll help for a while. Your hands are a mess as well as your forearms and knees, but overall, I think you will be fine."

After saddling up in the morning, José handed Colonel Woods the beat-up Winchester rifle he recovered from Indian Jake. "Colonel, thank you again for your help. This is Jake's rifle; I would like you to have it."

Woods stared at it for a minute before he could say anything. "José, I don't know what to say, this should be yours . . ."

"No, I have a rifle; you should have this one."

Woods nodded and took the rifle. "I will treasure it, thank you."

"Colonel, when you get back to the fort will you send a wire to my brother Andres at the railroad office in Magdalena telling them that I will be home soon?"

"Certainly, but wait just a moment before you leave." Walking to his horse he removed his binoculars and hung them on José's saddle. "Here is a replacement for your binoculars, and if something happens to these just let me know, I have more. Good luck with your new ranch, and take care, and no more chasing outlaws." Woods put out his hand to José. "I'm proud to know you Mister Taylor, you are a warrior . . ."

"Thank you Colonel, but Jake was the warrior, I just did my job. However, I have chased my last outlaw, I am now just José Taylor, horse and cattle rancher. Sal, this is for you, if you would like it," he said, handing him Jake's knife.

"Thank you boss, this is very good of you."

"Where are the rest of the hired hands?"

"I paid them off and let them go several days ago."

"That is good. You have proven to be a good man on the trail, I think you would make a good cow boss for my new ranch in Colorado."

"You have a ranch in Colorado too?"

"Yes. I am planning on moving when I get back. Would you like to work for me?"

" I would like that very much."

"Then it is settled. When we get back to Magdalena we will head for Colorado."

Chapter 20

José and Sal spent an extra day along the river at San Antonio giving the horses a rest. Both the men and horses were tired and sore from another long ride across the desert.

"Sal, how long have you been riding that old army saddle?"

"Oh, maybe ten years or so."

"Have you thought about a new one? One that may be more comfortable and not so worn out?"

"Sure, but I never had the money for a good one."

"When we get to the ranch you can pick out one of mine, I have several."

"Much appreciated boss, I could really use one." The next day they took the short ride to Socorro then rode the train to Magdalena. Andres met them as they were walking their horses out of the train car.

"So the Indian is dead?" he asked.

"Yes, it is over," said José. "How did you know that?"

"Deputy Rundle has put out the word. José, you are a hero."

"No, I am not a hero, I just did my job."

"Well, people here feel different about that, you will see."

After a good meal from Marisol, they rode to the sheriff's office. Don Rundle met them at the door. "Congratulations José, you finally got him! The territory is a safer place now that he's dead."

"Perhaps the territory is safer now," said José with a shrug. "But I believe I will miss what it was thirty years ago."

Rundle looked confused. "Aren't you pleased that he's dead? He killed a lot of people and even scalped some of them.

"I am just happy I no longer have to do this work." He handed the sheriff's badge to him and shook his hand. "The job is yours now, I am officially retired."

Riding into the ranch, Sara Song met him before he got to the barn. "Husband get down now, I need to touch you." Climbing down from the horse, she jumped into his arms and kissed him, unable to hold back the tears any longer. She held him tight and continued to kiss him. "Husband, please tell me that you did not get shot again."

"Wife, I did not get shot, just scratched up. I just need to rest before we leave for Colorado."

"Husband, you told me this was your last trip, please tell me you have not changed your mind."

"I have not, I am retired. Deputy Rundle is now wearing the sheriff's badge and I am just a rancher."

She kissed him one more time. "Okay husband, but before you have supper and lay down tonight to rest, you know what you must do . . ."

"No, I do not know what you are speaking of."

"You stink!"

"I thought the bathing tub was damaged in the storm?"

"Albert fixed it and it is ready to use."

After the morning meal, José went to the bunkhouse and found Scotty. "I came to pay you for your hat and shirt. I could not save the shirt but I have the hat even though it is somewhat worse for the wear. I want to pay you for what I damaged."

"Mister Taylor, I ain't worried about it none. Just working here the last few weeks has been great. Albert and Laura have been takin' good care of me and seem to have plenty of work. 'Sides, it looks like that old hat has a new bullet hole through it." He stuck his fingers through both holes. "Musta been quite a shootout."

José nodded. "Still, I need to make it right," said José, looking at the holes in the hat.

"Well, I've taken' a liken' to the one you traded me for. How 'bout we call it even?"

José shook his hand. "Even it is."

The family had a last meal together. Laura and Sara Song made frijoles, tamales, ham steak, potatoes and two kinds of bread. Homemade berry preserves and fresh milk, a rare treat, sat on the sideboard. The evening was spent talking in front of the fireplace and playing with little John.

*

Backing the wagon up to the cabin, everyone helped move their goods out of the cabin and said their goodbye's. Sara Song, José and Sal spent one last night with Andres and Marisol and in the morning, they loaded everything onto the train. "Goodbye brother," said José. "Please come to Colorado to see us."

"We will try, but you know how busy it is here. Wire us when you get there safely."

As the train pulled out, they settled in for the long ride. When they reached Trinidad, they stayed on the train while the passengers moved on and off. When they took on enough coal and water, the whistle blew and they started north. Reaching Colorado Springs, they stayed at a small hotel near the station and had a good meal of beef roast and boiled carrots.

The train left for Fairplay at 9:00 a.m. for the last leg of their trip. Reaching Fairplay by midafternoon, they stepped onto the platform and looked at the snowcapped mountains. "This is just about the most beautiful place I ever saw," said Sal.

A wagon pulled up to the platform and Deacon Roberts stepped out. "Howdy Mister Taylor, Missus Taylor. I don't think I met this fella here though."

"Deacon Roberts, this is my ranch foreman, Sal Bedford."

"Good to meet you Sal."

"Good to meet you too, Mister Roberts."

"Let's head for your ranch and get you settled in, I'm sure you're pretty tired from the trip."

The wagon pulled onto a long lane and up to the barn. The horses were in the corral and plenty of hay was laid in. The new cabin sat looking east with a view for miles. With the metal roofing that matched the barn and smoke coming out of the chimney, their new home looked exactly like she had hoped. It was up against the hills with a view looking out on South Park. In the back, a high rimrock ledge stood in front of a pair of snow-covered mountains called Buffalo Peaks. It was the most beautiful place she had ever seen.

Inside the cabin a fresh fire was laid and the windows even had curtains in place. "Courtesy of my wife," said Roberts. "She's excited to have another woman close by."

"Everything is very good Mister Roberts; you have done us a fine job. We can go to the bank in town and I can pay you now."

"We can go tomorrow if that is okay with you. My wife has made a meal in hopes that you might join us on your first night here."

"That is very good of you Mister Roberts," said Sara Song. "We would like very much to share a meal with you and your wife."

Over the next few days José bought a used four-hole stove and built a new bed for them. Sal would sleep in front of the fire for a few days until they finished building a small bunkhouse behind the barn. Little John still slept in the bed Albert built for him. José hung his Winchester above the mantel and laid his old deputy's badge and the spurs with one bent heel strap on it. The twisted mesquite cane went in the corner. When the bunkhouse was complete, they would build a bathing tub for Sara Song.

Looking out the window into the park, she motioned for José to join her.

"Husband, it is beautiful here, I am very happy. Do you think we will miss New Mexico?"

"I will miss seeing Andres and Marisol. I will miss Albert and Laura and the old ranch. But I will not miss New Mexico."

"Do you like Colorado more than New Mexico because it is more beautiful?"

He pulled her close and wrapped his arms around her. "New Mexico is also beautiful, but there are many things about it I would like to forget. In Colorado I have only you, John, the ranch, and the chance to make many good memories."

She took his hand and moved it to her stomach. "Husband, can you feel my belly?"

"Wife, I think you may be eating too much again."

She pulled his arms even tighter. "Husband, you know better. This is our daughter growing inside me."

"You seem very confident that it is a girl . . .

Acknowledgments

Like always, I lean heavily on those who so graciously offer to help me with the manuscript. Without them this would just be a bunch of words that wander aimlessly across the pages.

Nancy Entwistle, my bride of 53 years. She bravely reads and corrects, then reads and corrects again until it finally begins to look like a manuscript, I couldn't do it without her and I wouldn't want to.

Tim O'Byrne, Friend and editor for nearly 20 years. Many thanks for your support for all these years, enjoy that doctors degree.

Bob Baker, friend of 40 years. He reads everything for me, fixes my truck and puts up with my endless questions about the work. You are a brave guy and I appreciate you putting up with me all these years.

Greg Wood, my 4-wheeling pal. You read whatever I ask without question and give great feedback, no matter how many boring questions I ask. Many thanks for all your support and let's make a plan for a future trip.

Carol Morrell, my new friend and mystery lover. Thanks so much for your generous offer to be a test reader. It's a lot to take on and I can't thank you enough.

Lenetta and Gary Haynes, old friends and neighbors. Your feedback is always great and I get it from two points of view, that is invaluable. Hope you like westerns.

Bruce Flourquist, friend, reader and fellow book lover. Again, many thanks for your help on this project, your advise is important to me.

Don Kallaus, friend, partner on lots of projects and master book builder.

westernimages@msn.com

(719) 287-8063

www.ingramcontent.com/pod-product-compliance
Lightning Source LLC
Chambersburg PA
CBHW020636260626
47157CB00008B/2775